4. YOUNG YEARS LIBRARY

BEST LOVED STORIES AND POEMS

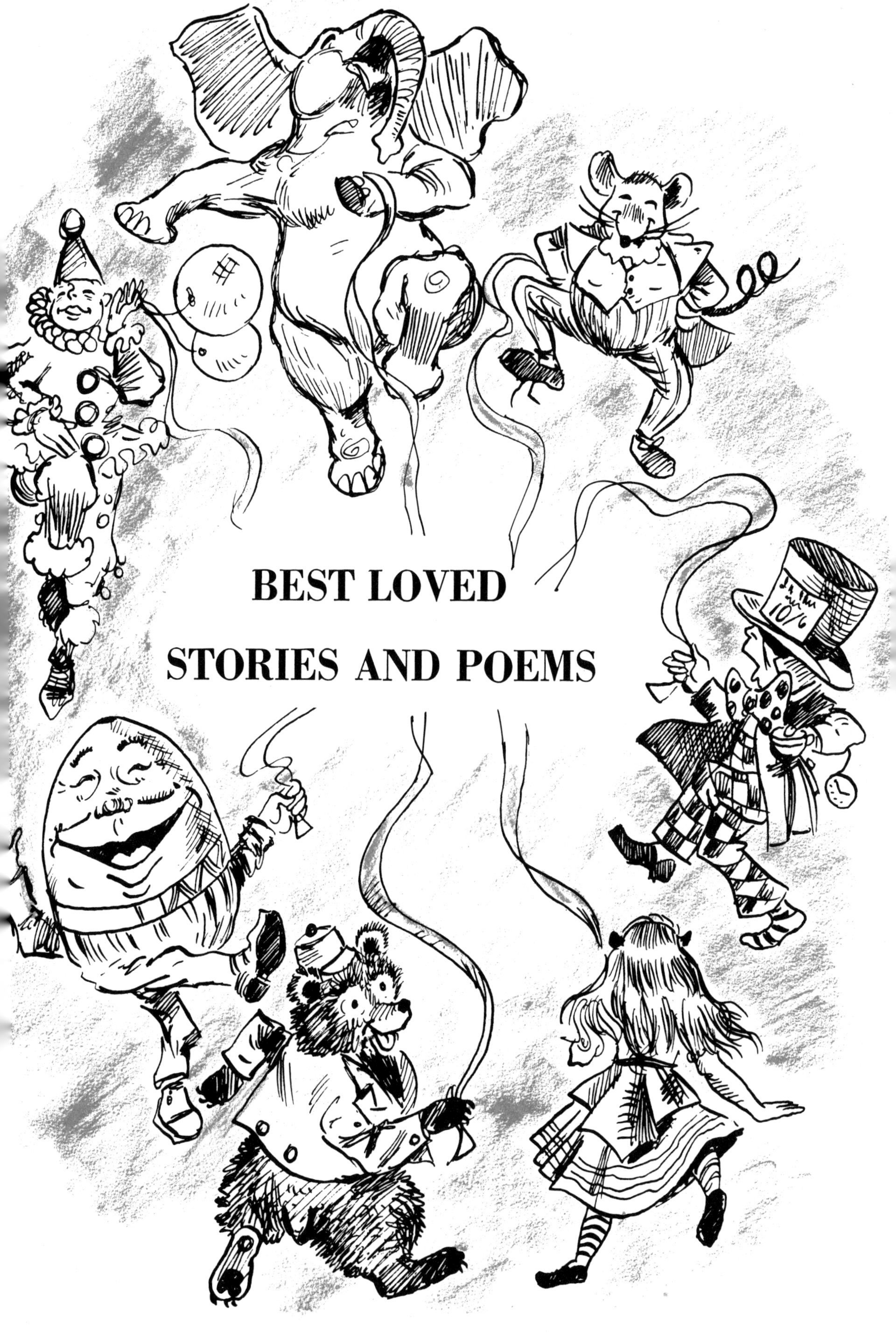

YOUNG

BEST LOVED
STORIES AND POEMS
FOR LITTLE CHILDREN

YEARS
LIBRARY

Editor

AUGUSTA BAKER

Coordinator of Children's Services

THE NEW YORK PUBLIC LIBRARY

Published By

PARENTS' CULTURAL INSTITUTE

A division of

Parents' Magazine Enterprises, Inc.

New York, N.Y.

Library of Congress Catalog Card No. 63-12348

MANUFACTURED IN THE UNITED STATES OF AMERICA
BY RAND McNALLY & COMPANY

PREFACE

In this volume of the *Young Years Library* we are introduced to favorite stories and poems on a somewhat older age level than those that appear in the previous volumes. As in the preceding ones, care has been maintained to preserve wherever possible the original classic illustrations. Parents may wish to impart interesting anecdotes about the authors of our selections to their children while reading them.

The first selection is from the classic childrens' book about Holland, *Hans Brinker; or the Silver Skates* by Mary Mapes Dodge. Here is a beautiful description of Holland of the early nineteenth century. When Mary Mapes Dodge wrote the book she had never even been in Holland; yet after it was published in 1865 the book was sold in the leading Dutch bookstores as the best guide available for tourists visiting that country.

Some children may not yet have made the acquaintance of Winnie-the-Pooh. But once they meet this lovable, silly, real-life teddy bear, they will take to him as Winnie-the-Pooh does to that jar of honey which figures so prominently in our selection "In Which Winnie-the-Pooh Goes Visiting and Gets Into a Tight Place." A. A. Milne's enchanting book "Winnie-the-Pooh" was originally published in 1926.

Where there are children's stories there must be a wicked witch, and the one lurking around the corner in this volume was created in the year 1900 by Lyman Frank Baum in *The Wonderful Wizard of Oz*. Baum wrote fourteen books about the land of Oz, yet it was the first of the series that so captured the imagination of children, not only in the United States, but in practically every country of the world. It is our hope that the story selected will encourage young readers to seek out the full book and all the other Oz books too. Actually, there are forty Oz books altogether, but twenty-six of these were written by various authors after Baum's death. It is of passing interest to learn that the 1939 motion picture extravaganza that starred Judy Garland as a singing Dorothy was preceded in 1925 by a silent film version in which the Tin Woodman was played by Oliver Hardy of the Laurel and Hardy comedy team.

There are two selections from the *Tom Sawyer* of Samuel L. Clemens, published under his pseudonym of Mark Twain in 1867. "The Glorious Whitewasher" details probably the most ingenious ruse ever devised by boy or man to get other people to do one's own chores, while in "Tom Takes Becky's Punishment" is enacted one of the most tender scenes of childhood affection found in literature.

Many of the fairy tales of the Brothers Grimm are included in earlier volumes of the *Young Years Library*. One has been saved for maturer minds in this volume: "The Cat And The Mouse In Partnership." The story of a sophisticated cat swindling a naive mouse and then gobbling him up is not exactly edifying, but then that is not the purpose of fairy tales.

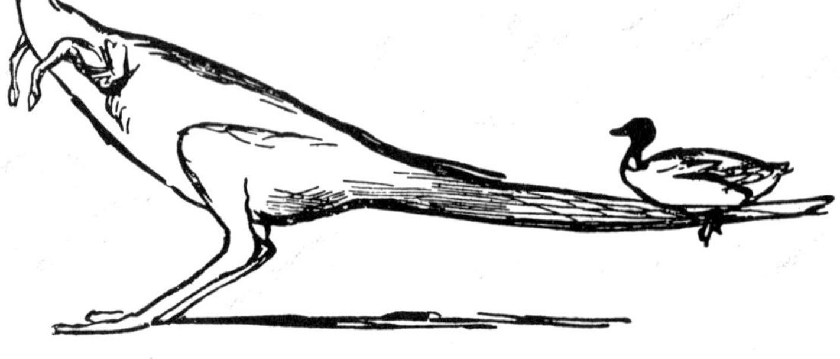

Traditionally in many homes, Christmas Eve comes to a splendid climax after the tree has been decorated and the family sits down to listen to father reading excerpts from Charles Dickens' immortal *A Christmas Carol.* More often than not, these excerpts are the result of years of trial-and-error endeavors to condense the whole story so that it can be read in one sitting. It is with warm pleasure, therefore, that we offer in this volume a little-known condensation of *A Christmas Carol,* abridged by Mr. Dickens himself for his own readings. Now, on a Christmas Eve, all of us will be able to read it aloud without surreptitiously skipping pages while no one is watching.

Nonsense and wisdom are more friends than foes, so it is not altogether unfitting that the wise witticisms of Mr. Benjamin Franklin should follow close upon the "Nonsense" verse of Mr. Edward Lear. And that is just where a selection of Ben Franklin's famous quotations appear, and the thoughts expresses in them are as apt today as they were a hundred years ago. They are presented here not with any didactic intent to instruct the young, but precisely because they *are* timely and they *are* fun.

A folk tale that has inspired prose, poetry and music is the *Sorcerer's Apprentice.* The tale was told eighteen hundred years ago by the Greek writer Lucian; it was immortalized in Goethe's poetry, recaptured in comparatively modern times by the music of Paul Dukas; and we present it in this volume in a beautiful story written by Richard Rostron.

Washington Irving's "Rip Van Winkle" — here presented in its entirety — is an Americanized version of another European folk tale. It was published in 1820 as part of Irving's *The Sketch Book.*

A relative newcomer as an acknowledged classic of children's literature is the "Wind In The Willows," written some fifty years ago but already a favorite everywhere. Kenneth Grahame wrote the book when he was the secretary of the Bank of England, having told it originally as bedtime stories to his son. When Grahame retired from the Bank of England, he also retired as a writer. He said he didn't need the money and he wanted to devote himself to the out-of-doors, just as his lovable River Rat, Mole, Badger and other river companions were accustomed to spend *their* time.

The reader will also recognize selections from such other great classics in this volume as *Swiss Family Robinson, Black Beauty* and *The Water Babies*. Then, of course, there are the immortal poems from the giants: Shakespeare, Longfellow, Browning, Emerson, Keats, Coleredge, Poe, among others, thereby truly earning this volume's title of "Best Loved Stories and Poems for Little Children."

Bradford Chambers
Coordinating Editor

ACKNOWLEDGMENTS

"The River Bank" is reprinted with the permission of Charles Scribner's Sons from THE WIND IN THE WILLOWS by Kenneth Grahame. Copyright 1908, 1933, 1953 by Charles Scribner's Sons.

"Animal Crackers" from SONGS FOR A LITTLE HOUSE by Christopher Morley. Copyright 1917, 1945 by Christopher Morley. Published by J. B. Lippincott Company.

"The Sorcerer's Apprentice" from THE SORCERER'S APPRENTICE by Richard Rostron. Illustrated by Frank Lieberman. Copyright 1941 by Richard Rostron by permission of William Morrow and Company, Inc.

Selection: "In Which Pooh Goes Visiting" from WINNIE-THE-POOH by A. A. Milne. Illustrated by E. H. Shepard. Copyright 1924 by E. P. Dutton & Co., Inc. Renewal, 1952 by A. A. Milne. Reprinted by permission of the publishers.

Illustrations, Designs and Layouts

Illustrated with original illustrations by Nicholas Amorosi, Oscar Liebman, John Lencicki, Kurt Werth, and reproductions of famous drawings and paintings by John Beer, Leslie Brooke, W. W. Denslow, Allen B. Doggett, Gustave Doré, Kate Greenaway, Edward Lear, Frank Lieberman, Ernest H. Shepherd, Linley Sambourne, George T. Tobin, Arthur Rackham *(as adapted by George Geygan)*. Designs and layouts by George Geygan, Morton Garchik, B. Shostick, Walter Bernard, Barbara Tanner, John Caggiano.

Art Directors

George Geygan
Morton Garchik

Cover, end,papers and title page: George Geygan

CONTENTS

ON THE CANAL 14
IN WHICH POOH
GOES VISITING AND
GETS INTO A TIGHT PLACE 24
MY EARLY HOME 30
THE SEARCH FOR THE WICKED
WITCH 38
THE GLORIOUS WHITEWASHER 56
TOM TAKES BECKY'S PUNISHMENT .. 66
THE CAT AND THE MOUSE IN
PARTNERSHIP 74
A CHRISTMAS CAROL 78
WISE SAYINGS FROM
POOR RICHARD 120
QUANGLE WANGLE'S HAT 126
THE SORCERER'S APPRENTICE 130
THE PIED PIPER OF HAMELIN 140
RIP VAN WINKLE 152
THE WRECK 175
THE DUCK AND THE KANGAROO 181

THE RIVER BANK 185
TOM BECOMES A WATER BABY 205
REEDS OF INNOCENCE 219
ANIMAL CRACKERS 220
THE VILLAGE BLACKSMITH 222
A TWISTER A-TWISTING 226
THE SPIDER AND THE FLY 228
THE RAVEN 231
THE SADDEST WORDS 243
THE YEAR'S AT THE SPRING 244
UNDER THE GREENWOOD TREE 245
A THING OF BEAUTY 246
HOW DO I LOVE THEE? 247
EPIGRAM 248
ON THE GRASSHOPPER AND THE CRICKET 249
FABLE 250
INDEX 251
INDEX FOR VOL. 1–4 252

STORIES

ON THE CANAL

From Hans Brinker, or The Silver Skates
By Mary Mapes Dodge

The setting of this children's story is Holland. It is about the youthful adventures of Dutch children. The chapter selected below describes some of their activities at the approach of St. Nicholas Day, the Dutch counterpart of our Christmas. The author of this story had never been to Holland before she wrote it; yet this has become more than a children's classic; soon after it was published —in 1865—it became the most popular guide book for tourists visiting Holland.

THE SKATING SEASON had commenced unusually early: our boys were by no means alone upon the ice. The afternoon was so fine that men, women and children, bent upon enjoying the holiday, had flocked to the grand canal from far and near. St. Nicholas had evidently remembered the favorite pastime: shining new skates were everywhere to be seen. Whole families were skimming their way to Haarlem, or Leyden, or the neighboring villages. The ice seemed fairly alive. Ben noticed the erect, easy carriage of the women, and their picturesque variety of costume. There were the latest fashions, fresh from Paris, floating past dingy, moth-eaten garments that had seen service through two generations; coal-scuttle bonnets perched over freckled faces bright with holiday smiles; stiff muslin caps, with wings at the sides, flapping beside cheeks rosy with health and contentment; furs, too, encircling the whitest of throats; and scanty garments fluttering below faces ruddy with exercise: in short, every quaint and comical mixture of dry-goods and flesh that Holland could furnish seemed sent to enliven the scene.

There were belles from Leyden, and fishwives from the border villages; cheese-women from Gouda, and prim matrons from beautiful country-seats on the Haarlemmer Meer. Grey-headed skaters were constantly to be seen; wrinkled old women with baskets upon their heads; and plump little toddlers on skates, clutching at their mother's gowns. Some women carried their babies upon their backs, firmly secured with a bright shawl. The effect was pretty and graceful as they darted by, or sailed slowly past, now nodding to an acquaintance, now chirruping, and throwing soft baby-talk, to the muffled little ones they carried.

Boys and girls were chasing each other, and hiding behind the one-horse sleds that, loaded high with peat or timber, pursued their cautious way along the track marked out as "safe." Beautiful, queenly women were there, enjoyment sparkling in their quiet eyes. Sometimes a long file of young men, each grasping the coat of the one before him, flew by with electric speed; and sometimes the ice squeaked under the chair of some gorgeous old dowager, or rich burgomaster's lady, who, very red in the nose and sharp in the eyes, looked like a scarethaw invented by old Father Winter for the protection of his skating grounds. The chair would be heavy with foot-stoves and cushions, to say nothing of the old lady. Mounted upon shining runners, it slid along, pushed by the sleepiest of servants, who, looking neither to the right nor the left, bent himself to his task, while she cast direful glances upon the screaming little rowdies who invariably acted as body-guard.

As for the men, they were pictures of placid enjoyment. Some were attired in ordinary citizen's dress; but many looked odd enough with their short woollen coats, wide breeches and big silver buckles. These seemed to Ben like little boys, who had, by a miracle, sprung suddenly into manhood, and were forced to wear garments that their astonished mothers had altered in a hurry. He noticed, too, that nearly all the men had pipes, as they passed him, whizzing and smoking like so many locomotives. There was every variety of pipes, from those of common clay to the most expensive meerschaums mounted in silver and gold. Some were carved into extraordinary and fantastic shapes, representing birds, flowers, heads, bugs and dozens of other things; some resembled the "Dutchman's pipe," that grows in our American woods; some were red, and many were of a pure, snowy white; but the most respectable were those which were ripening into a shaded brown. The deeper and richer the brown, of course, the more honored the pipe; for it was a proof that the owner, if honestly shading it, was deliberately devoting his manhood to the effort. What pipe would not be proud to be the object of such a sacrifice!

For a while, Ben skated on in silence. There was so much to engage his attention that he almost forgot his companions. Part of the time he had been watching the ice-boats as they flew over the great Haarlemmer Meer (or lake), the frozen surface of which was now plainly visible from the canal. These boats had very large sails,—much larger, in proportion, than those of ordinary vessels,—and were set upon a triangular frame, furnished with an iron "runner" at each corner; the widest part of the triangle crossing the bow, and its point stretching beyond the stern. They had rudders for

guiding, and brakes for arresting their progress; and were of all sizes and kinds, from small, rough affairs, managed by a boy, to large and beautiful ones filled with gay pleasure-parties, and manned by competent sailors, who, smoking their stumpy pipes, reefed and tacked and steered with great solemnity and precision.

Some of the boats were painted and gilded in gaudy style, and flaunted gay pennons from their mastheads; others, white as snow, with every spotless sail rounded by the wind, looked like swans borne onward by a resistless current. It seemed to Ben, as, following his fancy, he watched one of these in the distance, that he could almost hear its helpless, terrified cry; but he soon found that the sound arose from a nearer and less romantic cause,—from an ice-boat, not fifty yards from him, using its brakes to avoid a collision with a peat-sled.

It was a rare thing for these boats to be upon the canal; and their appearance generally caused no little excitement among skaters, especially among the timid: but to-day every ice-boat in the country seemed afloat, or, rather, aslide; and the canal had its full share.

Ben, though delighted at the sight, was often startled at the swift approach of the resistless, high-winged things, threatening to dart in any and every possible direction. It required all his energies to keep out of the way of the passers-by, and to prevent those screaming little urchins from upsetting him with their sleds. Once he halted to watch some boys who were making a hole in the ice, preparatory to using their fishing-spears. Just as he concluded to start again, he found himself suddenly bumped into an old lady's lap. Her push-chair had come upon him from the rear. The old lady screamed; the servant who was propelling her gave a warning hiss. In another instant Ben found himself apologizing to empty air: the indignant old lady was far ahead.

This was a slight mishap compared with one that now threatened him. A huge ice-boat, under full sail, came tearing down the canal, almost paralyzing Ben with the thought of instant destruction. It was close upon him. He saw its gilded prow, heard the *schipper* shout, felt the great boom fairly whiz over his head, was blind, deaf and dumb, all in an instant, then opened his eyes, to find himself spinning some

yards behind its great skate-like rudder. It had passed within an inch of his shoulder; but he was safe,—safe to see England again,—safe to kiss the dear faces that for an instant had flashed before him one by one,—father, mother, Robby and Jenny: that great boom had dashed their images into his very soul. He knew now how much he loved them. Perhaps this knowledge made him face complacently the scowls of those on the canal who seemed to feel that a boy in danger was necessarily a *bad* boy, needing instant reprimand.

Lambert chided him roundly.

"I thought it was all over with you, you careless fellow! Why don't you look where you are going? Not content with sitting on all the old ladies' laps, you must make a Juggernaut of every ice-boat that comes along. We shall have to hand you over to the *aanspreekers* yet, if you don't look out!"

"Please don't," said Ben, with mock humility; then, seeing how pale Lambert's lips were, added in a low tone,—

"I do believe I *thought* more in that one moment, Van Mounen, than in all the rest of my past life."

There was no reply; and, for a while, the two boys skated on in silence.

Soon a faint sound of distant bells reached their ears.

"Hark!" said Ben. "What is that?"

"The *carillons*," replied Lambert. "They are trying the bells in the chapel of yonder village. Ah, Ben! you should hear the chimes of the 'New Church' at Delft. They are superb,—nearly five hundred sweet-toned bells, and one of the best *carilloneurs* of Holland to play upon them. Hard work, though: they say the fellow often has to go to bed from positive exhaustion, after his performances. You see, the bells are attached to a kind of key-board, something like they have on piano-fortes: there are also a set of pedals for the feet. When a brisk tune is going on, the player looks like a kicking frog fastened to his seat with a skewer."

"For shame!" said Ben, indignantly.

Peter had, for the present, exhausted his stock of Haarlem anecdotes; and now, having nothing to do but to skate, he and his three companions were hastening to "catch up" with Lambert and Ben.

"That English lad is fleet enough," said Peter. "If he were a born Hollander, he could do no better. Generally these John Bulls make but a sorry figure on skates.—Halloo! Here you are, Van Mounen: why, we hardly hoped for the honor of meeting you again. Whom were you flying from in such haste?"

"Snails," retorted Lambert. "What kept you?"

"We have been talking; and, besides, we halted once to give Poot a.chance to rest."

"He begins to look rather worn out," said Lambert, in a low voice.

Just then a beautiful ice-boat, with reefed sail and flying streamers, swept leisurely by. Its deck was filled with children muffled up to their chins. Looking at them from the ice, you could see only smiling little faces embedded in bright-colored woollen wrappings. They were singing a chorus in honor of St. Nicholas. The music, starting in the discord of a hundred childish voices, floated, as it rose, into exquisite harmony:—

"Friend of sailors and of children,
Double claim have we,
As, in youthful joy, we're sailing
O'er a frozen sea.
Nicholas, St. Nicholas,
Let us sing to thee!

"While through wintry air we're rushing,
As our voices blend,
Are you near us? Do you hear us
Nicholas, our friend?
Nicholas, St. Nicholas,
Love can never end!

"Sunny sparkles, bright before us,
Chase away the cold;
Hearts where sunny thoughts are welcome
Never can grow old.
Nicholas, St. Nicholas,
Never can grow old!

"Pretty gift and loving lesson,
Festival and glee,
Bid us thank thee as we're sailing
O'er the frozen sea.
Nicholas, St. Nicholas,
So we sing to thee!"

In Which Pooh Goes Visiting and Gets Into a Tight Place

From Winnie-the-Pooh
By A. A. Milne

EDWARD BEAR, KNOWN to his friends as Winnie-the-Pooh, or Pooh for short, was walking through the forest one day, humming proudly to himself. He had made up a little hum that very morning, as he was doing his Stoutness Exercises in front of the glass: *Tra-la-la, tra-la-la,* as he stretched up as high as he could go, and then *Tra-la-la, tra-la—oh, help!—la,* as he tried to reach his toes. After breakfast he had said it over and over to himself until he had learnt it off by heart, and now he was humming it right through, properly. It went like this:

Tra-la-la, tra-la-la,
Tra-la-la, tra-la-la,
Rum-tum-tiddle-um-tum.
Tiddle-iddle, tiddle-iddle,
Tiddle-iddle, tiddle-iddle,
Rum-tum-tum-tiddle-um.

Well, he was humming this hum to himself, and walking along gaily, wondering what everybody else was doing, and what it felt like, being somebody else, when suddenly he came to a sandy bank, and in the bank was a large hole.

"Aha!" said Pooh. (*Rum-tum-tiddle-um-tum.*) "If I know anything about anything, that hole means Rabbit," he said, "and Rabbit means Company," he said, "and Company means Food and Listening-to-Me-Humming and such like. *Rum-tum-tum-tiddle-um.*"

So he bent down, put his head into the hole, and called out:

"Is anybody at home?"

There was a sudden scuffling noise from inside the hole, and then silence.

"What I said was, 'Is anybody at home?' " called out Pooh very loudly.

"No!" said a voice; and then added, "You needn't shout so loud. I heard you quite well the first time."

"Bother!" said Pooh. "Isn't there anybody here at all?"

"Nobody."

Winnie-the-Pooh took his head out of the hole, and thought for a little, and he thought to himself, "There must be somebody there, because somebody must have *said* 'Nobody.' " So he put his head back in the hole, and said:

"Hallo, Rabbit, isn't that you?"

"No," said Rabbit, in a different sort of voice this time.

"But isn't that Rabbit's voice?"

"I don't *think* so," said Rabbit. "It isn't *meant* to be."

"Oh!" said Pooh.

He took his head out of the hole, and had another think, and then he put it back, and said:

"Well, could you very kindly tell me where Rabbit is?"

"He has gone to see his friend Pooh Bear, who is a great friend of his."

"But this *is* Me!" said Bear, very much surprised.

"What sort of Me?"

"Pooh Bear."

"Are you sure?" said Rabbit, still more surprised.

"Quite, quite sure," said Pooh.

"Oh, well, then, come in."

So Pooh pushed and pushed and pushed his way through the hole, and at last he got in.

"You were quite right," said Rabbit, looking at him all over. "It *is* you. Glad to see you."

"Who did you think it was?"

"Well, I wasn't sure. You know how it is in the Forest. One can't have *anybody* coming into one's house. One has to be *careful*. What about a mouthful of something?"

Pooh always liked a little something at eleven o'clock in the morning, and he was very glad to see Rabbit getting out the plates and mugs; and when Rabbit said, "Honey or condensed milk with your bread?" he was so excited that he said, "Both," and then, so as not to seem greedy, he added, "But don't bother about the bread, please." And for a long time after that he said nothing . . . until at last, humming to himself in a rather sticky voice, he got up, shook Rabbit lovingly by the paw, and said that he must be going on.

"Must you?" said Rabbit politely.

"Well," said Pooh, "I could stay a little longer if it–if you——" and he tried very hard to look in the direction of the larder.

"As a matter of fact," said Rabbit, "I was going out myself directly."

"Oh, well, then, I'll be going on. Good-bye."

"Well, good-bye, if you're sure you won't have any more."

"*Is* there any more?" asked Pooh quickly.

Rabbit took the covers off the dishes, and said, "No, there wasn't."

"I thought not," said Pooh, nodding to himself. "Well, good-bye. I must be going on."

So he started to climb out of the hole. He pulled with his front paws, and pushed with his back paws, and in a little while his nose was out in the open again . . . and then his ears . . . and then his front paws . . . and then his shoulders . . . and then——

"Oh, help!" said Pooh. "I'd better go back."

"Oh, bother!" said Pooh. "I shall have to go on."

"I can't do either!" said Pooh. "Oh, help *and* bother!"

Now by this time Rabbit wanted to go for a walk too, and finding the front door full, he went out by the back door, and came around to Pooh, and looked at him.

"Hallo, are you stuck?" he asked.

"N-no," said Pooh carelessly. "Just resting and thinking and humming to myself."

"Here, give us a paw."

Pooh Bear stretched out a paw, and Rabbit pulled and pulled and pulled. . . .

"Ow!" cried Pooh. "You're hurting!"

"The fact is," said Rabbit, "you're stuck."

"It all comes," said Pooh crossly, "of not having front doors big enough."

"It all comes," said Rabbit sternly, "of eating too much. I thought at the time," said Rabbit, "only I didn't like to say anything," said Rabbit, "that one of us was eating too much," said Rabbit, "and I knew it wasn't *me,*" he said. "Well, well, I shall go and fetch Christopher Robin."

Christopher Robin lived at the other end of the Forest, and when he came back with Rabbit, and saw the front half of Pooh, he said, "Silly old Bear," in such a loving voice that everybody felt quite hopeful again.

"I was just beginning to think," said Bear, sniffing slightly,

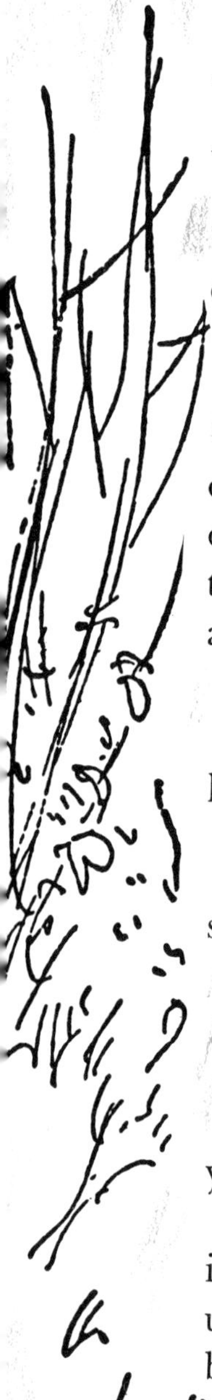

"that Rabbit might never be able to use his front door again. And I should *hate* that," he said.

"So should I," said Rabbit.

"Use his front door again?" said Christopher Robin. "Of course he'll use his front door again."

"Good," said Rabbit.

"If we can't pull you out, Pooh, we might push you back."

Rabbit scratched his whiskers thoughtfully, and pointed out that, when once Pooh was pushed back, he was back, and of course nobody was more glad to see Pooh than *he* was, still there it was, some lived in trees and some lived underground, and——

"You mean I'd *never* get out?" said Pooh.

"I mean," said Rabbit, "that having got *so* far, it seems a pity to waste it."

Christopher Robin nodded.

"Then there's only one thing to be done," he said. "We shall have to wait for you to get thin again."

"How long does getting thin take?" asked Pooh anxiously.

"About a week, I should think."

"But I can't stay here for a *week!*"

"You can *stay* here all right, silly old Bear. It's getting you out which is so difficult."

"We'll read to you," said Rabbit cheerfully. "And I hope it won't snow," he added. "And I say, old fellow, you're taking up a good deal of room in my house—*do* you mind if I use your back legs as a towel-horse? Because, I mean, there they are—

doing nothing—and it would be very convenient just to hang the towels on them."

"A week!" said Pooh gloomily. *"What about meals?"*

"I'm afraid no meals," said Christopher Robin, "because of getting thin quicker. But we *will* read to you."

Bear began to sigh, and then found he couldn't because he was so tightly stuck; and a tear rolled down his eye, as he said:

"Then would you read a Sustaining Book, such as would help and comfort a Wedged Bear in Great Tightness?"

So for a week Christopher Robin read that sort of book at the North end of Pooh, and Rabbit hung his washing on the South end . . . and in between Bear felt himself getting slenderer and slenderer. And at the end of the week Christopher Robin said, *"Now!"*

So he took hold of Pooh's front paws and Rabbit took hold of Christopher Robin, and all Rabbit's friends and relations took hold of Rabbit, and they all pulled together. . . .

And for a long time Pooh only said *"Ow!"* . . .

And *"Oh!"* . . .

And then, all of a sudden, he said *"Pop!"* just as if a cork were coming out of a bottle.

And Christopher Robin and Rabbit and all Rabbit's friends and relations went head-over-heels backwards . . . and on the top of them came Winnie-the-Pooh—free!

So, with a nod of thanks to his friends, he went on with his walk through the forest, humming proudly to himself. But, Christopher Robin looked after him lovingly, and said to himself, "Silly old Bear!"

My Early Home

From Black Beauty
By Anna Sewell

THE first place that I can well remember, was a large pleasant meadow with a pond of clear water in it. Some shady trees leaned over it, and rushes and water-lilies grew at the deep end. Over the hedge on one side we looked into a ploughed field, and on the other we looked over a gate at our master's house, which stood by the roadside; at the top of the meadow was a plantation of fir trees, and at the bottom a running brook overhung by a steep bank.

Whilst I was young I lived upon my mother's milk, as I could not eat grass. In the day time I ran by her side, and at night I lay down close by her. When it was hot, we used to stand by the pond in the shade of the trees, and when it was cold, we had a nice warm shed near the plantation.

As soon as I was old enough to eat grass, my mother used to go out to work in the day time, and came back in the evening.

There were six young colts in the meadow besides me; they were older than I was; some were nearly as large as grown-up horses. I used to run with them, and had great fun; we used to gallop all together round and round the field, as hard as we could go. Sometimes we had rather rough play, for they would frequently bite and kick as well as gallop.

One day, when there was a good deal of kicking, my mother whinnied to me to come to her, and then she said,—

"I wish you to pay attention to what I am going to say to you. The colts who live here are very good colts, but they are cart horse colts, and, of course, they have not learned manners. You have been well bred and well born; your father has a great name in these parts, and your grandfather won the cup two years at the Newmarket races; your grandmother had the sweetest temper of any horse I ever knew, and I think you have never seen me kick or bite. I hope you will grow up gentle and good, and never learn bad ways; do your work with a good will, lift your feet up well when you trot, and never bite or kick even in play."

I have never forgotten my mother's advice; I knew she was a wise old horse, and our master thought a great deal of her. Her name was Duchess, but he often called her Pet.

Our master was a good, kind man. He gave us good food, good lodging, and kind words; he spoke as kindly to us as he did to his little children. We were all fond of him, and my mother loved him very much. When she saw him at the gate, she would neigh with joy, and trot up to him. He would pat and stroke her and say, "Well, old Pet, and how is your little Darkie?" I was a dull black, so he called me Darkie; then he would give me a piece of bread, which was very good, and sometimes he brought a carrot for my mother. All the horses

would come to him, but I think we were his favourites. My mother always took him to the town on a market day in a light gig.

There was a ploughboy, Dick, who sometimes came into our field to pluck blackberries from the hedge. When he had eaten all he wanted, he would have, what he called, fun with the colts, throwing stones and sticks at them to make them gallop. We did not much mind him, for we could gallop off; but sometimes a stone would hit and hurt us.

One day he was at this game, and did not know that the master was in the next field; but he was there, watching what was going on; over the hedge he jumped in a snap, and catching Dick by the arm, he gave him such a box on the ear as made him roar with the pain and surprise. As soon as we saw the master, we trotted up nearer to see what went on.

"Bad boy!" he said, "bad boy! to chase the colts. This is not the first time, nor the second, but it shall be the last—there—take your money and go home, I shall not want you on my farm again." So we never saw Dick any more. Old Daniel, the man who looked after the horses, was just as gentle as our master, so we were well off.

I was now beginning to grow handsome; my coat had grown fine and soft, and was bright black. I had one white foot, and a pretty white star on my forehead. I was thought very handsome; my master would not sell me till I was four years old; he said lads ought not to work like men, and colts ought not to work like horses till they were quite grown up.

When I was four years old, Squire Gordon came to look at me. He examined my eyes, my mouth, and my legs; he felt them all down; and then I had to walk and trot and gallop before him; he seemed to like me, and said, "When he has been well broken in, he will do very well." My master said he would break me in himself, as he should not like me to be frightened or hurt, and he lost no time about it, for the next day he began.

Every one may not know what breaking in is, therefore I will describe it. It means to teach a horse to wear a saddle and bridle and to carry on his back a man, woman, or child; to go just the way they wish, and to go quietly. Besides this, he has to learn to wear a collar, a crupper, and a breeching, and to stand still whilst they are put on; then to have a cart or a chaise fixed behind him, so that he cannot walk or trot without dragging it after him: and he must go fast or slow, just as his driver wishes. He must never start at what he sees, nor speak to other horses, nor bite, nor kick, nor have any will of his own; but always do his master's will, even though

he may be very tired or hungry; but the worst of all is, when his harness is once on, he may neither jump for joy nor lie down for weariness. So you see this breaking in is a great thing.

I had of course long been used to a halter and a headstall, and to be led about in the fields and lanes quietly, but now I was to have a bit and bridle; my master gave me some oats as usual, and after a good deal of coaxing, he got the bit into my mouth, and the bridle fixed, but it was a nasty thing! Those who have never had a bit in their mouths cannot think how bad it feels; a great piece of cold hard steel as thick as a man's finger to be pushed into one's mouth, between one's teeth and over one's tongue, with the ends coming out at the corner of your mouth, and held fast there by straps over your head, under your throat, round your nose, and under your chin; so that no way in the world can you get rid of the nasty hard thing; it is very bad! yes, very bad! at least I thought so; but I knew my mother always wore one when she went out, and all horses did when they were grown up; and so, what with the nice oats, and what with my master's pats, kind words, and gentle ways, I got to wear my bit and bridle.

Next came the saddle, but that was not half so bad; my master put it on my back very gently, whilst old Daniel held my head; he then made the girths fast under my body, patting and talking to me all the time; then I had a few oats, then a little leading about, and this he did every day till I began to look for the oats and the saddle. At length one morning, my master got on my back and rode me round the meadow on the soft grass. It certainly did feel queer; but I must say I felt rather proud to carry my master, and as he continued to ride me a little every day, I soon became accustomed to it.

The next unpleasant business was putting on the iron shoes; that too was very hard at first. My master went with me to the smith's forge, to see that I was not hurt or got any fright. The blacksmith took my feet in his hand one after the other and cut away some of the hoof. It did not pain me, so I stood still on three legs till he had done them all. Then he took a piece of iron the shape of my foot, and clapped it on, and drove some nails through the shoe quite into my hoof, so that the shoe was firmly on. My feet felt very stiff and heavy, but in time I got used to it.

And now having got so far, my master went on to break me to harness; there were more new things to wear. First, a stiff heavy collar just on my neck, and a bridle with great side-

pieces against my eyes called blinkers, and blinkers indeed they were, for I could not see on either side, but only straight in front of me; next there was a small saddle with a nasty stiff strap that went right under my tail; that was the crupper. I hated the crupper—to have my long tail doubled up and poked through that strap was almost as bad as the bit. I never felt more like kicking, but of course I could not kick such a good master, and so in time I got used to everything, and could do my work as well as my mother.

I must not forget to mention one part of my training, which I have always considered a very great advantage. My master sent me for a fortnight to a neighbouring farmer's, who had a meadow which was skirted on one side by the railway. Here were some sheep and cows, and I was turned in amongst them.

I shall never forget the first train that ran by. I was feeding quietly near the pales which separated the meadow from the railway, when I heard a strange sound at a distance, and before I knew whence it came—with a rush and a clatter, and a puffing out of smoke—a long black train of something flew by, and was gone almost before I could draw my breath. I turned, and galloped to the further side of the meadow as fast as I could go, and there I stood snorting with astonishment and fear. In the course of the day many other trains went by, some more slowly; these drew up at the station close by, and sometimes made an awful shriek and groan before they stopped. I thought it very dreadful, but the cows went on eating very quietly, and hardly raised their heads as the black frightful thing came puffing and grinding past.

For the first few days I could not feed in peace; but as I found that this terrible creature never came into the field, or did me any harm, I began to disregard it, and very soon I cared as little about the passing of a train as the cows and sheep did.

Since then I have seen many horses much alarmed and restive at the sight or sound of a steam engine; but thanks to my good master's care, I am as fearless at railway stations as in my own stable.

Now if any one wants to break in a young horse well, that is the way.

My master often drove me in double harness with my mother, because she was steady, and could teach me how to go better than a strange horse. She told me the better I behaved, the better I should be treated, and that it was wisest always to do my best to please my master; "but," said she, "there are a great many kinds of men; there are good, thoughtful men like our master, that any horse may be proud to serve; but there are bad, cruel men, who never ought to have a horse or dog to call their own. Beside, there are a great many foolish men, vain, ignorant, and careless, who never trouble themselves to think; these spoil more horses than all, just for want of sense; they don't mean it, but they do it for all that. I hope you will fall into good hands; but a horse never knows who may buy him, or who may drive him; it is all a chance for us, but still I say, do your best wherever it is, and keep up your good name."

THE SEARCH FOR THE WICKED WITCH

From The Wonderful Wizard of Oz
by L. FRANK BAUM

Little Dorothy and her companions—the straw scarecrow, the tin woodsman and the cowardly lion—have just had their audience with the Wizard of Oz. Each has made a wish: Dorothy, that she be returned to her home in Kansas; the scarecrow has asked for a brain; the tin woodsman, a heart; and the lion, courage. They have been told that their wishes will be granted on the condition that they kill the Wicked Witch of the West.

THE SOLDIER with the green whiskers led them through the streets of the Emerald City until they reached the room where the Guardian of the Gates lived. This officer unlocked their spectacles to put them back in his great box, and then he politely opened the gate for our friends.

"Which road leads to the Wicked Witch of the West?" asked Dorothy.

"There is no road," answered the Guardian of the Gates; "no one ever wishes to go that way."

"How, then, are we to find her?" enquired the girl.

"That will be easy," replied the man; "for when she knows you are in the Country of the Winkies she will find you, and make you all her slaves."

"Perhaps not," said the Scarecrow, "for we mean to destroy her."

"Oh, that is different," said the Guardian of the Gates. "No one has ever destroyed her before, so I naturally thought she would make slaves of you, as she has of all the rest. But take care; for she is wicked and fierce, and may not allow you to destroy her. Keep to the West, where the sun sets, and you cannot fail to find her."

OZ

They thanked him and bade him goodbye, and turned toward the West, walking over the fields of soft grass dotted here and there with daisies and buttercups. Dorothy still wore the pretty silk dress she had put on in the palace, but now, to her surprise, she found it was no longer green, but pure white. The ribbon around Toto's neck had also lost its green color and was as white as Dorothy's dress.

The Emerald City was soon left far behind. As they advanced the ground became rougher and hillier, for there were no farms nor houses in this country of the West, and the ground was untilled.

In the afternoon the sun shone hot in their faces, for there were no trees to offer them shade; so that before night Dorothy and Toto and the Lion were tired, and lay down upon the grass and fell asleep, with the Woodman and the Scarecrow keeping watch.

Now the Wicked Witch of the West had but one eye, yet that was as powerful as a telescope, and could see everywhere. So, as she sat in the door of her castle, she happened to look around and saw Dorothy lying asleep, with her friends all about her. They were a long distance off, but the Wicked Witch was angry to find them in her country; so she blew upon a silver whistle that hung around her neck.

At once there came running to her from all directions a pack of great wolves. They had long legs and fierce eyes and sharp teeth.

"Go to those people," said the Witch, "and tear them to pieces."

"Are you not going to make them your slaves?" asked the leader of the wolves.

"No," she answered, "one is of tin, and one of straw; one is a girl and another a Lion. None of them is fit to work, so you may tear them into small pieces."

"Very well," said the wolf, and he dashed away at full speed, followed by the others.

It was lucky the Scarecrow and the Woodman were wide awake and heard the wolves coming.

"This is my fight," said the Woodman; "so get behind me and I will meet them as they come."

He seized his axe, which he had made very sharp, and as the leader of the wolves came on the Tin Woodman swung his arm and chopped the wolf's head from its body, so that it immediately died. As soon as he could raise his axe another wolf came up, and he also fell under the sharp edge of the Tin Woodman's weapon. There were forty wolves, and forty times a wolf was killed; so that at last they all lay dead in a heap before the Woodman.

Then he put down his axe and sat beside the Scarecrow, who said,

"It was a good fight, friend."

They waited until Dorothy awoke the next morning. The little girl was quite frightened when she saw the great pile of shaggy wolves, but the Tin Woodman told her all. She thanked him for saving them and sat down to breakfast, after which they started again upon their journey.

Now this same morning the Wicked Witch came to the door of her castle and looked out with her one eye that could see afar off. She saw all her wolves lying dead, and the strangers still travelling through her country. This made her angrier than before, and she blew her silver whistle twice.

Straightway a great flock of wild crows came flying toward her, enough to darken the sky. And the Wicked Witch said to the King Crow,

"Fly at once to the strangers; peck out their eyes and tear them to pieces."

The wild crows flew in one great flock toward Dorothy and her companions. When the little girl saw them coming she was afraid. But the Scarecrow said,

"This is my battle; so lie down beside me and you will not be harmed."

So they all lay upon the ground except the Scarecrow, and he stood up and stretched out his arms. And when the crows saw him they were frightened, as these birds always are by scarecrows, and did not dare to come any nearer. But the King Crow said,

"It is only a stuffed man. I will peck his eyes out."

The King Crow flew at the Scarecrow, who caught it by the head and twisted its neck until it died. And then another crow flew at him, and the Scarecrow twisted its neck also. There were forty crows, and forty times the Scarecrow twisted a neck, until at last all were lying dead beside him. Then he

called to his companions to rise, and again they went upon their journey.

When the Wicked Witch looked out again and saw all her crows lying in a heap, she got into a terrible rage, and blew three times upon her silver whistle.

Forthwith there was heard a great buzzing in the air, and a swarm of black bees came flying towards her.

"Go to the strangers and sting them to death!" commanded the Witch, and the bees turned and flew rapidly until they came to where Dorothy and her friends were walking. But the Woodman had seen them coming and the Scarecrow had decided what to do.

"Take out my straw and scatter it over the little girl and the dog and the lion," he said to the Woodman, "and the bees cannot sting them." This the Woodman did, and as Dorothy lay close beside the Lion and held Toto in her arms, the straw covered them entirely.

The bees came and found no one but the Woodman to sting, so they flew at him and broke off all their stings against the tin, without hurting the Woodman at all. And as bees cannot live when their stings are broken that was the end of the black bees, and they lay scattered thick about the Woodman, like little heaps of fine coal.

Then Dorothy and the Lion got up, and the girl helped the Tin Woodman put the straw back into the Scarecrow again, until he was as good as ever. So they started upon their journey once more.

The Wicked Witch was so angry when she saw her black bees in little heaps like fine coal that she stamped her foot and tore her hair and gnashed her teeth. And then she called a dozen of her slaves, who were the Winkies, and gave them sharp spears, telling them to go to the strangers and destroy them.

The Winkies were not a brave people, but they had to do as they were told; so they marched away until they came near to Dorothy. Then the Lion gave a great roar and sprang toward them, and the poor Winkies were so frightened that they ran back as fast as they could.

When they returned to the castle the Wicked Witch beat them well with a strap, and sent them back to their work, after which she sat down to think what she should do next. She could not understand how all her plans to destroy these strangers had failed; but she was a powerful Witch, as well as a wicked one, and she soon made up her mind how to act.

There was, in her cupboard, a Golden Cap, with a circle of diamonds and rubies running round it. This Golden Cap had a charm. Whoever owned it could call three times upon the Winged Monkeys, who would obey any order they were given. But no person could command these strange creatures more than three times. Twice already the Wicked Witch had used the charm of the Cap. Once was when she had made the Winkies her slaves, and set herself to rule over their country. The Winged Monkeys had helped her do this. The second time was when she had fought against the Great Oz himself, and driven him out of the land of the West. The Winged Monkeys had also helped her in doing this. Only once more could she use this Golden Cap, for which reason she did not like to do so until all her other powers were exhausted. But now that her fierce wolves and her wild crows and her stinging bees were gone, and her slaves had been scared away by the Cowardly Lion, she saw there was only one way left to destroy Dorothy and her friends.

So the Wicked Witch took the Golden Cap from her cupboard and placed it upon her head. Then she stood upon her left foot and said, slowly,

"Ep-pe, pep-pe, kak-ke!"

Next she stood upon her right foot and said,

"Hil-lo, hol-lo, hel-lo!"

After this she stood upon both feet and cried in a loud voice,

"Ziz-zy, zuz-zy, zik!"

Now the charm began to work. The sky was darkened, and a low rumbling sound was heard in the air. There was a rushing of many wings; a great chattering and laughing; and the sun came out of the dark sky to show the Wicked Witch surrounded by a crowd of monkeys, each with a pair of immense and powerful wings on his shoulders.

One, much bigger than the others, seemed to be their leader. He flew close to the Witch and said,

"You have called us for the third and last time. What do you command?"

"Go to the strangers who are within my land and destroy them all except the Lion," said the Wicked Witch. "Bring that beast to me, for I have a mind to harness him like a horse, and make him work."

"Your commands shall be obeyed," said the leader; and then, with a great deal of chattering and noise, the Winged Monkeys flew away to the place where Dorothy and her friends were walking.

Some of the Monkeys seized the Tin Woodman and carried him through the air until they were over a country thickly covered with sharp rocks. Here they dropped the poor Woodman, who fell a great distance to the rocks, where he lay so battered and dented that he could neither move nor groan.

Others of the Monkeys caught the Scarecrow, and with their long fingers pulled all of the straw out of his clothes and head. They made his hat and boots and clothes into a small bundle and threw it into the top branches of a tall tree.

The remaining Monkeys threw pieces of stout rope around the Lion and wound many coils about his body and head and legs, until he was unable to bite or scratch or struggle in any way. Then they lifted him up and flew away with him to the Witch's castle, where he was placed in a small yard with a high iron fence around it, so that he could not escape.

But Dorothy they did not harm at all. She stood, with Toto in her arms, watching the sad fate of her comrades and thinking it would soon be her turn. The leader of the Winged Monkeys flew up to her, his long, hairy arms stretched out and his ugly face grinning terribly; but he saw the mark of the Good Witch's kiss upon her forehead and stopped short, motioning the others not to touch her.

"We dare not harm this little girl," he said to them, "for she is protected by the Power of Good, and that is greater than the Power of Evil. All we can do is to carry her to the castle of the Wicked Witch and leave her there."

So, carefully and gently, they lifted Dorothy in their arms and carried her swiftly through the air until they came to the castle, where they set her down upon the front door step. Then the leader said to the Witch,

"We have obeyed you as far as we were able. The Tin

Woodman and the Scarecrow are destroyed, and the Lion is tied up in your yard. The little girl we dare not harm, nor the dog she carries in her arms. Your power over our band is now ended, and you will never see us again."

Then all the Winged Monkeys, with much laughing and chattering and noise, flew into the air and were soon out of sight.

The Wicked Witch was both surprised and worried when she saw the mark on Dorothy's forehead, for she knew well that neither the Winged Monkeys nor she, herself, dare hurt the girl in any way. She looked down at Dorothy's feet, and seeing the Silver Shoes, began to tremble with fear, for she knew what a powerful charm belonged to them. At first the Witch was tempted to run away from Dorothy; but she happened to look into the child's eyes and saw how simple the soul behind them was, and that the little girl did not know of the wonderful power the Silver Shoes gave her. So the Wicked Witch laughed to herself, and thought, "I can still make her my slave, for she does not know how to use her power." Then she said to Dorothy, harshly and severely,

"Come with me; and see that you mind everything I tell you, for if you do not I will make an end of you, as I did of the Tin Woodman and the Scarecrow."

Dorothy followed her through many of the beautiful rooms in her castle until they came to the kitchen, where the Witch bade her clean the pots and kettles and sweep the floor and keep the fire fed with wood.

Dorothy went to work meekly, with her mind made up to work as hard as she could; for she was glad the Wicked Witch had decided not to kill her.

With Dorothy hard at work the Witch thought she would go into the court-yard and harness the Cowardly Lion like a horse; it would amuse her, she was sure, to make him draw her chariot whenever she wished to go to drive. But as she opened the gate the Lion gave a loud roar and bounded at her so fiercely that the Witch was afraid, and ran out and shut the gate again.

"If I cannot harness you," said the Witch to the Lion, speaking through the bars of the gate, "I can starve you. You shall have nothing to eat until you do as I wish."

So after that she took no food to the imprisoned Lion; but every day she came to the gate at noon and asked,

"Are you ready to be harnessed like a horse?"

And the Lion would answer,

"No. If you come in this yard I will bite you."

The reason the Lion did not have to do as the Witch wished was that every night, while the woman was asleep, Dorothy carried him food from the cupboard. After he had eaten he would lie down on his bed of straw, and Dorothy would lie beside him and put her head on his soft, shaggy mane, while they talked of their troubles and tried to plan some way to escape. But they could find no way to get out of the castle, for it was constantly guarded by the yellow Winkies, who were the slaves of the Wicked Witch and too afraid of her not to do as she told them.

The girl had to work hard during the day, and often the Witch threatened to beat her with the same old umbrella she always carried in her hand. But, in truth, she did not dare to strike Dorothy, because of the mark upon her forehead. The child did not know this, and was full of fear for herself and Toto. Once the Witch struck Toto a blow with her umbrella and the brave little dog flew at her and bit her leg, in return. The Witch did not bleed where she was bitten, for she was so wicked that the blood in her had dried up many years before.

Dorothy's life became very sad as she grew to understand that it would be harder than ever to get back to Kansas and Aunt Em again. Sometimes she would cry bitterly for hours, with Toto sitting at her feet and looking in her face, whining dismally to show how sorry he was for his little mistress. Toto did not really care whether he was in Kansas or the Land of Oz so long as Dorothy was with him; but he knew the little girl was unhappy, and that made him unhappy too.

Now the Wicked Witch had a great longing to have for her own the Silver Shoes which the girl always wore. Her Bees and her Crows and her Wolves were lying in heaps and drying up, and she had used up all the power of the Golden Cap; but if she could only get hold of the Silver Shoes they would give her more power than all the other things she had lost. She watched Dorothy carefully, to see if she ever took off her shoes,

thinking she might steal them. But the child was so proud of her pretty shoes that she never took them off except at night and when she took her bath. The Witch was too much afraid of the dark to dare go in Dorothy's room at night to take the shoes, and her dread of water was greater than her fear of the dark, so she never came near when Dorothy was bathing. Indeed, the old Witch never touched water, nor ever let water touch her in any way.

But the wicked creature was very cunning, and she finally thought of a trick that would give her what she wanted. She placed a bar of iron in the middle of the kitchen floor, and then by her magic arts made the iron invisible to human eyes. So that when Dorothy walked across the floor she stumbled over the bar, not being able to see it, and fell at full length. She was not much hurt, but in her fall one of the Silver Shoes came off, and before she could reach it the Witch had snatched it away and put it on her own skinny foot.

The wicked woman was greatly pleased with the success of her trick, for as long as she had one of the shoes she owned half the power of their charm, and Dorothy could not use it against her, even had she known how to do so.

The little girl, seeing she had lost one of her pretty shoes, grew angry, and said to the Witch,

"Give me back my shoe!"

"I will not," retorted the Witch, "for it is now my shoe, and not yours."

"You are a wicked creature!" cried Dorothy. "You have no right to take my shoe from me."

"I shall keep it, just the same," said the Witch, laughing at her, "and some day I shall get the other one from you, too."

This made Dorothy so very angry that she picked up the bucket of water that stood near and dashed it over the Witch, wetting her from head to foot.

Instantly the wicked woman gave a loud cry of fear; and

then, as Dorothy looked at her in wonder, the Witch began to shrink and fall away.

"See what you have done!" she screamed. "In a minute I shall melt away."

"I'm very sorry, indeed," said Dorothy, who was truly frightened to see the Witch actually melting away like brown sugar before her very eyes.

"Didn't you know water would be the end of me?" asked the Witch, in a wailing, despairing voice.

"Of course not," answered Dorothy; "how should I?"

"Well, in a few minutes I shall be all melted, and you will have the castle to yourself. I have been wicked in my day, but I never thought a little girl like you would ever be able to melt me and end my wicked deeds. Look out—here I go!"

With these words the Witch fell down in a brown, melted, shapeless mass and began to spread over the clean boards of the kitchen floor. Seeing that she had really melted away to nothing, Dorothy drew another bucket of water and threw it over the mess. She then swept it all out the door. After picking out the silver shoe, which was all that was left of the old woman, she cleaned and dried it with a cloth, and put it on her foot again. Then, being at last free to do as she chose, she ran out to the court-yard to tell the Lion that the Wicked Witch of the West had come to an end, and that they were no longer prisoners in a strange land.

THE GLORIOUS WHITEWASHER

From the Adventures of Tom Sawyer
By Mark Twain

SATURDAY MORNING WAS come, and all the summer world was bright and fresh, and brimming with life. There was a song in every heart; and if the heart was young the music issued at the lips. There was cheer in every face and a spring in every step. The locust trees were in bloom and the fragrance of the blossoms filled the air. Cardiff Hill, beyond the village and above it, was green with vegetation, and it lay just far enough away to seem a Delectable Land, dreamy, reposeful, and inviting.

Tom appeared on the sidewalk with a bucket of whitewash and a long-handled brush. He surveyed the fence, and all gladness left him and a deep melancholy settled down upon his spirit. Thirty yards of board fence nine feet high. Life to him seemed hollow, and existence but a burden. Sighing he dipped his brush and passed it along the topmost plank; repeated the operation; did it again; compared the insignificant whitewashed streak with the far-reaching continent of unwhitewashed fence, and sat down on a tree-box discouraged. Jim came skipping out at the gate with a tin pail, and singing "Buffalo Gals." Bringing water from the town pump had always been hateful work in Tom's eyes, before, but now it did not strike him so. He remembered that there was company at the pump. White, mulatto, and negro boys and girls were always there waiting their turns, resting, trading playthings, quarreling, fighting, skylarking. And he remembered that although the pump was only a hundred and fifty yards off, Jim never got back with a bucket of water under an hour—and even then somebody generally had to go after him. Tom said:

"Say, Jim, I'll fetch the water if you'll whitewash some."

Jim shook his head and said:

"Can't, Mars Tom. Ole missis, she tole me I got to go an' git dis water an' not stop foolin' roun' wid anybody. She say she spec' Mars Tom gwine to ax me to whitewash, an' so she tole me go 'long an' 'tend to my own business—she 'lowed *she'd* 'tend to de whitewashin'."

"Oh, never you mind what she said, Jim. That's the way she always talks. Gimme the bucket—I won't be gone only a minute. *She* won't ever know."

"Oh, I dasn't, Mars Tom. Ole missis she'd take an' tar de head off'n me. 'Deed she would."

"*She!* She never licks anybody—whacks 'em over the head with her thimble—and who cares for that, I'd like to know. She talks awful, but talk don't hurt—anyways it don't if she don't cry. Jim, I'll give you a marvel. I'll give you a white alley!"

Jim began to waver.

"White alley, Jim! And it's a bully taw."

"My! Dat's a mighty gay marvel, *I* tell you! But Mars Tom I's powerful 'fraid ole missis—"

"And besides, if you will I'll show you my sore toe."

Jim was only human—this attraction was too much for him. He put down his pail, took the white alley, and bent over the toe with absorbing interest, while the bandage was being unwound. In another moment he was flying down the street with his pail and a tingling rear, Tom was white-washing with vigor, and Aunt Polly was retiring from the field with a slipper in her hand and triumph in her eye.

But Tom's energy did not last. He began to think of the fun he had planned for this day, and his sorrows multiplied. Soon the free boys would come tripping along on all sorts of delicious expeditions, and they would make a world of fun of him for having to work—the very thought of it burnt him like fire. He got out his worldly wealth and examined it—bits of toys, marbles, and trash; enough to buy an exchange of *work,* maybe, but not half enough to buy so much as half an hour of pure freedom. So he returned his straitened means to his pocket, and gave up the idea of trying to buy the boys. At this dark and hopeless moment an inspiration burst upon him! Nothing less than a great, magnificent inspiration.

He took up his brush and went tranquilly to work. Ben Rogers hove in sight presently—the very boy, of all boys, whose ridicule he had been dreading. Ben's gait was the hop-skip-and-jump—proof enough that his heart was light and his anticipations high. He was eating an apple, and giving a long, melodious whoop, at intervals, followed by a deep-toned ding-dong-dong, ding-dong-dong, for he was personating a steam-boat. As he drew near, he slackened speed, took the middle of the street, leaned far over to starboard and rounded to ponderously and with laborious pomp and circumstance—for he was personating the *Big Missouri,* and considered himself to be drawing nine feet of water. He was boat and captain and engine-bells combined, so he had to imagine himself standing on his own hurricane-deck giving the orders and executing them:

"Stop her, sir! Ting-a-ling-ling!" The headway ran almost out and he drew up slowly toward the sidewalk.

"Ship up to back! Ting-a-ling-ling!" His arms straightened and stiffened down his sides.

"Set her back on the stabboard! Ting-a-ling-ling! Chow! ch-chow-wow! Chow!" His right hand, meantime, describing stately circles—for it was representing a forty-foot wheel.

"Let her go back on the labboard! Ting-a-ling-ling! Chow-ch-chow-chow!" The left hand began to describe circles.

"Stop the stabboard! Ting-a-ling-ling! Stop the labboard! Come ahead on the stabboard! Stop her! Let your outside turn over slow! Ting-a-ling-ling! Chow-ow-ow! Get out that head-line! *Lively* now! Come—out with your spring-line—what're you about there! Take a turn round that stump with the bight of it! Stand by that stage, now—let her go! Done with the engines, sir! Ting-a-ling-ling! *Sh't! s'h't! sh't!* (trying the gauge-cocks).

Tom went on whitewashing—paid no attention to the steamboat. Ben stared a moment and then said:

"Hi-*yi! You're* up a stump, ain't you!"

No answer. Tom surveyed his last touch with the eye of an artist, then he gave his brush another gentle sweep and surveyed the result, as before. Ben ranged up alongside of him. Tom's mouth watered for the apple, but he stuck to his work. Ben said:

"Hello, old chap, you got to work, hey?"

Tom wheeled suddenly and said:

"Why, it's you, Ben! I warn't noticing."

"Say—*I*'m going in a-swimming, *I* am. Don't you wish you could? But of course you'd druther *work*—wouldn't you? Course you would!"

Tom contemplated the boy a bit, and said:

"What do you call work?"

"Why, ain't *that* work?"

Tom resumed his whitewashing, and answered carelessly:

"Well, maybe it is, and maybe it ain't. All I know, is, it suits Tom Sawyer."

"Oh come, now, you don't mean to let on that you *like* it?"

The brush continued to move.

"Like it? Well, I don't see why I oughtn't to like it. Does a boy get a chance to whitewash a fence every day?"

That put the thing in a new light. Ben stopped nibbling his apple. Tom swept his brush daintily back and forth —stepped back to note the effect—added a touch here and

there—criticized the effect again—Ben watching every move and getting more and more interested, more and more absorbed. Presently he said:

"Say, Tom, let *me* whitewash a little."

Tom considered, was about to consent; but he altered his mind:

"No—no—I reckon it wouldn't hardly do, Ben. You see, Aunt Polly's awful particular about this fence—right here on the street, you know—but if it was the back fence I wouldn't mind and *she* wouldn't. Yes, she's awful particular about this fence; it's got to be done very careful; I reckon there ain't one boy in a thousand, maybe two thousand, that can do it the way it's got to be done."

"No—is that so? Oh come, now—lemme just try. Only just a little—I'd let *you,* if you was me, Tom."

"Ben, I'd like to, honest injun; but Aunt Polly—well, Jim wanted to do it, but she wouldn't let him; Sid wanted to do it, and she wouldn't let Sid. Now don't you see how I'm fixed? If you was to tackle this fence and anything was to happen to it—"

"Oh, shucks, I'll be just as careful. Now lemme try. Say—I'll give you the core of my apple."

"Well, here— No, Ben, now don't. I'm afeard—"

"I'll give you *all* of it!"

Tom gave up the brush with reluctance in his face, but alacrity in his heart. And while the late steamer *Big Missouri* worked and sweated in the sun, the retired artist sat on a barrel in the shade close by, dangled his legs, munched his apple, and planned the slaughter of more innocents. There was no lack of material; boys happened along every little while; they came to jeer, but remained to whitewash. By the time Ben was fagged out, Tom had traded the next chance to Billy Fisher for a kite, in good repair; and when *he* played out, Johnny Miller bought in for a dead rat and a string to swing it with—and so on, and so on, hour after hour. And when the middle of the afternoon came, from being a poor poverty-stricken boy in the morning, Tom was literally rolling in wealth. He had beside the things before mentioned, twelve marbles, part of a jews'-harp, a piece of blue bottle-glass to look through, a spool cannon, a key that wouldn't unlock anything, a fragment of chalk, a glass stopper of a decanter, a tin soldier, a couple of tadpoles, six firecrackers, a kitten with only one eye, a brass door-knob, a dog-collar—but no dog—the handle of a knife, four pieces of orange-peel, and a dilapidated old window-sash.

He had had a nice, good, idle time all the while—plenty of company—and the fence had three coats of whitewash on it! If he hadn't run out of whitewash, he would have bankrupted every boy in the village.

Tom said to himself that it was not such a hollow world, after all. He had discovered a great law of human action, without knowing it—namely, that in order to make a man or a boy covet a thing, it is only necessary to make the thing difficult to attain. If he had been a great and wise philosopher, like the writer of this book, he would now have comprehended that Work consists of whatever a body is *obliged* to do, and that Play consists of whatever a body is not obliged to do. And this would help him to understand why constructing artificial flowers or performing on a treadmill is work, while rolling tenpins or climbing Mont Blanc is only amusement. There are wealthy gentlemen in England who drive four-horse passenger-coaches twenty or thirty miles on a daily line, in the summer, because the privilege costs them considerable money; but if they were offered wages for the service, that would turn it into work and then they would resign.

The boy mused awhile over the substantial change which had taken place in his worldly circumstances, and then wended toward headquarters to report.

Tom Takes Becky's Punishment

THERE WAS SOMETHING about Aunt Polly's manner, when she kissed Tom, that swept away his low spirits and made him light-hearted and happy again. He started to school and had the luck of coming upon Becky Thatcher at the head of Meadow Lane. His mood always determined his manner. Without a moment's hesitation he ran to her and said:

"I acted mighty mean to-day, Becky, and I'm so sorry. I won't ever, ever do that way again, as long as ever I live—please make up, won't you?"

The girl stopped and looked him scornfully in the face:

"I'll thank you to keep yourself *to* yourself, Mr. Thomas Sawyer. I'll never speak to you again."

She tossed her head and passed on. Tom was so stunned that he had not even presence of mind enough to say "Who cares, Miss Smarty?" until the right time to say it had gone by. So he said nothing. But he was in a fine rage, nevertheless. He moped into the schoolyard wishing she were a boy, and imagining how he would trounce her if she were. He presently encountered her and delivered a stinging remark as he passed. She hurled one in return, and the angry breach was complete. It seemed to Becky, in her hot resentment, that she could hardly wait for school to "take in," she was so impatient to see Tom flogged for the injured spellingbook. If she had had any lingering notion of exposing Alfred Temple, Tom's offensive fling had driven it entirely away.

Poor girl, she did not know how fast she was nearing trouble herself. The master, Mr. Dobbins, had reached middle age with an unsatisfied ambition. The darling of his desires was to be a doctor, but poverty had decreed that he should be nothing higher than a village schoolmaster. Every day he took a mysterious book out of his desk and absorbed himself in it at times when no classes were reciting. He kept that book under lock and key. There was not an urchin in school but was perishing to have a glimpse of it, but the chance never came. Every boy and girl had a theory about the nature of that book; but no two theories were alike, and

there was no way of getting at the facts in the case. Now, as Becky was passing by the desk, which stood near the door, she noticed that the key was in the lock! It was a precious moment. She glanced around; found herself alone, and the next instant she had the book in her hands. The title-page—Professor Somebody's *Anatomy*—carried no information to her mind; so she began to turn the leaves. She came at once upon a handsomely engraved and colored frontispiece—a human figure, stark naked. At that moment a shadow fell on the page and Tom Sawyer stepped in at the door, and caught a glimpse of the picture. Becky snatched at the book to close it, and had the hard luck to tear the pictured plate half down the middle. She thrust the volume into the desk, turned the key, and burst out crying with shame and vexation.

"Tom Sawyer, you are just as mean as you can be, to sneak up on a person and look at what they're looking at."

"How could *I* know you was looking at anything?"

"You ought to be ashamed of yourself, Tom Sawyer; you know you're going to tell on me, and oh, what shall I do, what shall I do! I'll be whipped, and I never was whipped in school."

Then she stamped her little foot and said:

"*Be* so mean if you want to! *I* know something that's going to happen. You just wait and you'll see! Hateful, hateful, hateful!"—and she flung out of the house with a new explosion of crying.

Tom stood still, rather flustered by this onslaught. Presently he said to himself:

"What a curious kind of a fool a girl is. Never been licked in school! Shucks. What's a licking! That's just like a girl—they're so thin-skinned and chicken-hearted. Well, of course *I* ain't going to tell old Dobbins on this little fool, because there's other ways of getting even on her that ain't so mean; but what of it? Old Dobbins will ask who it was tore his book. Nobody'll answer. Then he'll do just the way he always does—ask first one and then t'other, and when he comes to the right girl he'll know it, without any telling. Girls' faces always tell on them. They ain't got any backbone. She'll get licked. Well, it's a kind of a tight place for Becky Thatcher, because there ain't any way out of it." Tom conned the thing a moment longer and then added: "All right, though; she'd like to see me in just such a fix—let her sweat it out!"

Tom joined the mob of skylarking scholars outside. In a few moments the master arrived and school "took in." Tom did not feel a strong interest in his studies. Every time he stole a glance at the girls' side of the room Becky's face troubled him. Considering all things, he did not want to pity her, and yet it was all he could do to help it. He could get up no exultation that was really worthy the name. Presently the spelling-book discovery was made, and Tom's mind was entirely full of his own matters for a while after that. Becky roused up from her lethargy of distress and showed good interest in the proceedings. She did not expect that Tom could get out of his trouble by denying that he spilt the ink on the book himself; and she was right. The denial only seemed to make the thing worse for Tom. Becky supposed she would be glad of that, and she tried to believe she was glad of it, but she found she was not certain. When the worst came to the worst, she had an impulse to get up and tell on Alfred Temple, but she made an effort and forced herself to keep still—because, said she to herself, "he'll tell about me tearing the picture sure. I wouldn't say a word, not to save his life!"

Tom took his whipping and went back to his seat not at all broken-hearted, for he thought it was possible that he had unknowingly upset the ink on the spelling-book himself, in some skylarking bout—he had denied it for form's sake and because it was custom, and had stuck to the denial from principle.

A whole hour drifted by, the master sat nodding in his throne, the air was drowsy with the hum of study. By and by, Mr. Dobbins straightened himself up, yawned, then unlocked his desk, and reached for his book, but seemed undecided whether to take it out or leave it. Most of the pupils glanced up languidly, but there were two among them that watched his movements with intent eyes. Mr. Dobbins fingered his book absently for a while, then took it out and settled himself in his chair to read! Tom shot a glance at Becky. He had seen a hunted and helpless rabbit look as she did, with a gun leveled at its head. Instantly he forgot his quarrel with her. Quick—something must be done! done in a flash, too! But the very imminence of the emergency paralyzed his invention. Good!—he had an inspiration! He would run and snatch the book, spring through the door and fly. But his resolution shook for one little instant, and the chance was lost—the master opened the volume. If Tom only had the wasted opportunity back again! Too late. There was no help for Becky now, he said. The next moment the master faced the school. Every eye sank under his gaze. There was that in it which smote even the innocent with fear. There was silence while one might count ten, the master was gathering his wrath. Then he spoke:

"Who tore this book?"

There was not a sound. One could have heard a pin drop. The stillness continued; the master searched face after face for signs of guilt.

"Benjamin Rogers, did you tear this book?"

A denial. Another pause.

"Joseph Harper, did you?"

Another denial. Tom's uneasiness grew more and more intense under the slow torture of these proceedings. The master scanned the ranks of boys—considered awhile, then turned to the girls:

"Amy Lawrence?"

A shake of the head.

"Gracie Miller?"

The same sign.

"Susan Harper, did you do this?"

Another negative. The next girl was Becky Thatcher. Tom was trembling from head to foot with excitement and a sense of the hopelessness of the situation.

"Rebecca Thatcher" [Tom glanced at her face—it was white with terror]—"did you tear—no, look me in the face" [her hands rose in appeal]—"did you tear this book?"

A thought shot like lightning through Tom's brain. He sprang to his feet and shouted—"*I* done it!"

The school stared in perplexity at this incredible folly. Tom stood a moment, to gather his dismembered faculties; and when he stepped forward to go to his punishment the surprise, the gratitude, the adoration that shone upon him out of poor Becky's eyes seemed pay enough for a hundred floggings. Inspired by the splendor of his own act, he took without an outcry the most merciless flaying that even Mr. Dobbins had ever administered; and also received with indifference the added cruelty of a command to remain two hours after school should be dismissed—for he knew who would wait for him outside till his captivity was done, and not count the tedious time as loss, either.

Tom went to bed that night planning vengeance against Alfred Temple; for with shame and repentance Becky had told him all, not forgetting her own treachery; but even the longing for vengeance had to give way, soon, to pleasanter musings, and he fell asleep at last, with Becky's latest words lingering dreamily in his ear—

"Tom, how *could* you be so noble!"

THE CAT AND THE MOUSE IN PARTNERSHIP

A CAT once made the acquaintance of a Mouse, and she said so much to it about her love and friendship that at last the Mouse agreed to go into partnership and live together with her.

"We must take precautions for the winter," said the Cat, "or we shall suffer from hunger. You, little Mouse, dare not venture everywhere, and in the end you will get me into a scrape."

So the good advice was followed, and a pot of fat was purchased. They did not know where to keep it, but, after much deliberation, the Cat said, "I know no place where it would be safer than in the church; nobody dare venture to take anything there. We will put it under the altar, and will not touch it till we are obliged to."

So the pot was deposited in safety; but, before long, the Cat began to hanker after it, and said to the Mouse:

"Oh, little Mouse, my cousin has asked me to be godmother. She has brought a son into the world. He is white, with brown spots; and I am to hold him at the font. Let me go out to-day, and you stay alone to look after the house."

"Oh yes," said the Mouse, "for goodness sake, go; and if you have anything nice to eat, think of me. I would gladly have a drop of sweet raspberry wine myself."

Now there wasn't a word of truth in all this. The Cat had no cousin, and she had not been invited to be godmother at all. She went straight to the church, crept to the pot of fat, and began to lick it, and she licked and licked the whole of the top off it. Then she took a stroll on the house-tops and reflected on her proceedings, after which she stretched herself in the sun, and wiped her whiskers every time she thought of the pot of fat. She did not go home till evening.

"Oh, there you are again," said the Mouse; "you must have had a merry time."

"Oh, well enough," answered the Cat.

"What kind of name was given to the child?" asked the Mouse.

"Top-off," answered the Cat, drily.

"Top-off!" cried the Mouse. "What an extraordinary name; is it a common one in your family?"

"What does it matter?" said the Cat. "It's not worse than crumbstealers, as your godchildren are called."

Not long after,the Cat was again overcome by her desires. She said to the Mouse, "You must oblige me again by looking after the house alone. For the second time, I have been asked to be sponsor, and, as the child has a white ring round its neck, I can't refuse."

The good little Mouse was quite ready to oblige, and the Cat stole away behind the city walls to the church, and ate half of the pot of fat. "Nothing tastes better," she said, "than what one eats by oneself"; and she was quite satisfied with her day's work. When she got home, the Mouse asked what this child had been named.

"Half-gone."

"What do you say? I have never heard such a name in my life. I don't believe you would find it in the calendar."

Soon the Cat's mouth watered again for the dainty morsel.

"Good things always come in threes," she said to the Mouse; "again I am to stand sponsor. This child is quite black, with big white paws, but not another white hair on its body. Such a thing only occurs once in a few years. You will let me go out again, won't you?"

"Top-off! Half-gone! They are such curious names; they set me thinking."

"You sit at home in your dark grey velvet coat," said the Cat, "getting your head full of fancies. It all comes of not going out in the daytime."

During the Cat's absence, the Mouse cleared up and made the house tidy; but the greedy Cat ate up all the fat. "When it's all gone, one can be at peace," said she to herself, as she went home, late at night, fat and satiated.

The Mouse immediately asked what name had been given to the third child.

"I don't suppose it will please you any better," said the Cat. "He is called All-gone!"

"All-gone!" exclaimed the Mouse. "I have never seen it in print, All-gone! What is the meaning of it?"

She shook her head, rolled herself up, and went to sleep.

From this time nobody asked the Cat to be sponsor. But when the winter came, and it grew very difficult to get food, the Mouse remembered their store, and said, "Come, Cat, we will go to our pot of fat which we have saved up; won't it be good now?"

"Yes, indeed!" answered the Cat; "it will do you just as much good as putting your tongue out of the window."

They started off to the church, and when they got there, they found the fat-pot still in its place, but it was quite empty.

"Alas," said the Mouse, "now I see it all. Everything has come to the light of day. You have indeed been a true friend! You ate it all up when you went to be godmother. First Top-off, then Half-gone, then——"

"Hold your tongue," cried the Cat. "Another word, and I'll eat you too."

The unfortunate Mouse had "All-gone" on its lips, but hardly had it come out than the Cat made a spring, seized the Mouse, and gobbled it up.

Now, that's the way of the world, you see.

A Christmas Carol

By Charles Dickens
As condensed by Charles Dickens for his own readings

MARLEY'S GHOST

MARLEY WAS DEAD, to begin with. There is no doubt whatever about that. The register of his burial was signed by the clergyman, the clerk, the undertaker, and the chief mourner. Scrooge signed it. And Scrooge's name was good upon 'Change for anything he chose to put his hand to.

Old Marley was as dead as a door-nail.

Scrooge knew he was dead? Of course he did. How could it be otherwise? Scrooge and he were partners for I don't know how many years. Scrooge was his sole executor, his sole administrator, his sole assign, his sole residuary legatee, his sole friend, his sole mourner.

Scrooge never painted out old Marley's name, however. There it yet stood, years afterwards, above the warehouse door,—Scrooge and Marley. The firm was known as Scrooge and Marley. Sometimes people new to the business called Scrooge Scrooge, and sometimes Marley. He answered to both names. It was all the same to him.

Oh! But he was a tight-fisted hand at the grindstone, was Scrooge! a squeezing, wrenching, grasping, scraping, clutching, covetous old sinner! External heat and cold had little influence on him. No warmth could warm, no cold could chill him. No wind that blew was bitterer than he, no falling snow was more intent upon its purpose, no pelting rain less open to entreaty. Foul weather didn't know where to have him. The heaviest rain and snow and hail and sleet could boast of the advantage over him in only one respect,—they often "came down" handsomely, and Scrooge never did.

Nobody ever stopped him in the street to say, with gladsome looks, "My dear Scrooge, how are you? When will you come to see me?" No beggars implored him to bestow a trifle, no children asked him what it was o'clock, no man or woman ever once in all his life inquired the way to such and such a place, of Scrooge. Even the blindmen's dogs appeared to know him; and when they saw him coming on, would tug their owners into doorways and up courts; and then would wag their tails as though they said, "No eye at all is better than an evil eye, dark master!"

But what did Scrooge care! It was the very thing he liked. To edge his way along the crowded paths of life, warning all human sympathy to keep its distance, was what the knowing ones call "nuts" to Scrooge.

Once upon a time—of all the good days in the year, upon a Christmas eve—old Scrooge sat busy in his counting-house. It was cold, bleak, biting, foggy weather; and the city clocks had only just gone three, but it was quite dark already.

The door of Scrooge's counting-house was open, that he might keep his eye upon his clerk, who, in a dismal little cell beyond, a sort of tank, was copying letters. Scrooge had a very small fire, but the clerk's fire was so very much smaller that it looked like one coal. But he couldn't replenish it, for Scrooge kept the coal-box in his own room; and so surely as the clerk came in with the shovel, the master predicted that it would be necessary for them to part. Wherefore the clerk put on his white comforter, and tried to warm himself at the candle; in which effort, not being a man of a strong imagination, he failed.

"A merry Christmas, uncle! God save you!" cried a cheerful voice. It was the voice of Scrooge's nephew, who came upon him so quickly that this was the first intimation Scrooge had of his approach.

"Bah!" said Scrooge; "humbug!"

"Christmas a humbug, uncle! You don't mean that, I am sure?"

"I do. Out upon merry Christmas! What's Christmas time to you but a time for paying bills without money; a time for finding yourself a year older, and not an hour richer; a time for balancing your books and having every item in 'em through a round dozen of months presented dead against you? If I had my will, every idiot who goes about with 'Merry Christmas' on his lips should be boiled with his own pudding, and buried with a stake of holly through his heart. He should!"

"Uncle!"

"Nephew, keep Christmas in your own way, and let me keep it in mine."

"Keep it! But you don't keep it."

"Let me leave it alone, then. Much good may it do you! Much good it has ever done you!"

"There are many things from which I might have derived good, by which I have not profited, I dare say, Christmas among the rest. But I am sure I have always thought of Christmas time, when it has come round,—apart from the veneration due to its sacred origin, if anything belonging to it *can* be apart from that,—as a good time; a kind, forgiving, charitable, pleasant time; the only time I know of, in the long calendar of the year, when men and women seem by one consent to open their shut-up hearts freely, and to think of people below them as if they really were fellow-travellers to the grave, and not another race of creatures bound on other journeys. And therefore, uncle, though it has never put a scrap of gold or silver in my pocket, I believe that it *has* done me good, and *will* do me good; and I say, God bless it!"

The clerk in the tank involuntarily applauded.

"Let me hear another sound from *you,*" said Scrooge, "and you'll keep your Christmas by losing your situation! You're quite a powerful speaker, sir," he added, turning to his nephew. "I wonder you don't go into Parliament."

"Don't be angry, uncle. Come! Dine with us to-morrow."

Scrooge said that he would see him—yes, indeed he did. He went the whole length of the expression, and said that he would see him in that extremity first.

"But why?" cried Scrooge's nephew. "Why?"

"Why did you get married?"

"Because I fell in love."

"Because you fell in love!" growled Scrooge, as if that were the only one thing in the world more ridiculous than a merry Christmas. "Good afternoon!"

"Nay, uncle, but you never came to see me before that happened. Why give it as a reason for not coming now?"

"Good afternoon."

"I want nothing from you; I ask nothing of you; why cannot we be friends?"

"Good afternoon."

"I am sorry, with all my heart, to find you so resolute. We have never had any quarrel, to which I have been a party. But I have made the trial in homage to Christmas, and I'll keep my Christmas humor to the last. So A Merry Christmas, uncle!"

"Good afternoon!"

"And A Happy New Year!"

"Good afternoon!"

His nephew left the room without an angry word, notwithstanding. The clerk, in letting Scrooge's nephew out, had let two other people in. They were portly gentlemen, pleasant to behold, and now stood, with their hats off, in Scrooge's office. They had books and papers in their hands, and bowed to him.

"Scrooge and Marley's, I believe," said one of the gentlemen, referring to his list. "Have I the pleasure of addressing Mr. Scrooge, or Mr. Marley?"

"Mr. Marley has been dead these seven years. He died seven years ago, this very night."

"At this festive season of the year, Mr. Scrooge," said the gentleman, taking up a pen, "it is more than usually desirable that we should make some slight provisions for the poor and destitute, who suffer greatly at the present time. Many thousands are in want of common necessaries; hundreds of thousands are in want of common comforts, sir."

"Are there no prisons?"

"Plenty of prisons. But under the impression that they scarcely furnish Christian cheer of mind or body to the unoffending multitude, a few of us are endeavoring to raise a fund to buy the poor some meat and drink, and means of warmth. We choose this time, because it is a time, of all others, when Want is keenly felt, and Abundance rejoices. What shall I put you down for?"

"Nothing!"

"You wish to be anonymous?"

"I wish to be left alone. Since you ask me what I wish, gentlemen, that is my answer. I don't make merry myself at Christmas, and I can't afford to make idle people merry. I help to support the prisons and the workhouses,—they cost enough, —and those who are badly off must go there."

"Many can't go there; and many would rather die."

"If they would rather die, they had better do it, and decrease the surplus population."

At length the hour of shutting up the counting-house arrived. With an ill-will Scrooge, dismounting from his stool, tacitly admitted the fact to the expectant clerk in the tank, who instantly snuffed his candle out, and put on his hat.

"You'll want all day to-morrow, I suppose?"

"If quite convenient, sir."

"It's not convenient, and it's not fair. If I was to stop half a crown for it, you'd think yourself mightily ill-used, I'll be bound?"

"Yes, sir."

"And yet you don't think *me* ill-used, when I pay a day's wages for no work."

"It's only once a year, sir."

"A poor excuse for picking a man's pocket every twenty-fifth of December! But I suppose you must have the whole day. Be here all the earlier *next* morning."

The clerk promised that he would; and Scrooge walked out with a growl. The office was closed in a twinkling, and the clerk, with the long ends of his white comforter dangling below his waist (for he boasted no great-coat), went down a slide, at the end of a lane of boys, twenty times, in honor of its being Christmas eve, and then ran home as hard as he could pelt, to play at blindman's-buff.

Scrooge took his melancholy dinner in his usual melancholy tavern; and having read all the newspapers, and beguiled the rest of the evening with his banker's book, went home to bed. He lived in chambers which had once belonged to his deceased partner. They were a gloomy suite of rooms, in a lowering pile of building up a yard. The building was old enough now, and dreary enough; for nobody lived in it but Scrooge, the other rooms being all let out as offices.

Now it is a fact, that there was nothing at all particular about the knocker on the door of this house, except that it was very large; also, that Scrooge had seen it, night and morning, during his whole residence in that place; also, that Scrooge had as little of what is called fancy about him as any man in the city of London. And yet Scrooge, having his key in the lock of the door, saw in the knocker, without its undergoing any intermediate process of change, not a knocker, but Marley's face.

Marley's face, had a dismal light about it, like a bad lobster in a dark cellar. It was not angry or ferocious, but it looked at Scrooge as Marley used to look,—with ghostly spectacles turned up upon its ghostly forehead.

As Scrooge looked fixedly at this phenomenon, it was a knocker again. He said, "Pooh, pooh!" and closed the door with a bang.

The sound resounded through the house like thunder. Every room above, and every cask in the wine-merchant's cellars below, appeared to have a separate peal of echoes of its own. Scrooge was not a man to be frightened by echoes. He fastened the door, and walked across the hall, and up the stairs. Slowly too, trimming his candle as he went.

Up Scrooge went, not caring a button for its being very dark. Darkness is cheap, and Scrooge liked it. But before he shut his heavy door, he walked through his rooms to see that all was right. He had just enough recollection of the face to desire to do that.

Sitting-room, bedroom, lumber-room, all as they should be. Nobody under the table, nobody under the sofa; a small fire in the grate; spoon and basin ready; and the little saucepan of gruel (Scrooge had a cold in his head) upon the hob. Nobody under the bed; nobody in the closet; nobody in his dressing-gown, which was hanging up in a suspicious attitude against the wall. Lumber-room as usual. Old fire-guard, old shoes, two fish-baskets, washing-stand on three legs, and a poker.

Quite satisfied, he closed his door, and locked himself in; double-locked himself in, which was not his custom. Thus secured against surprise, he took off his cravat, put on his dressing-gown and slippers and his nightcap, and sat down before the very low fire to take his gruel.

As he threw his head back in the chair, his glance happened to rest upon a bell, a disused bell, that hung in the room, and communicated, for some purpose now forgotten, with a chamber in the highest story of the building. It was with great astonishment, and with a strange, inexplicable dread, that, as he looked, he saw this bell begin to swing. Soon

it rang out loudly, and so did every bell in the house.

This was succeeded by a clanking noise, deep down below, as if some person were dragging a heavy chain over the casks in the wine-merchant's cellar.

Then he heard the noise much louder, on the floors below; then coming up the stairs; then coming straight towards his door.

It came on through the heavy door, and a spectre passed into the room before his eyes. And upon its coming in, the dying flame leaped up, as though it cried, "I know him! Marley's ghost!"

The same face, the very same. Marley in his pigtail, usual waistcoat, tights, and boots. His body was transparent; so that Scrooge, observing him, and looking through his waistcoat, could see the two buttons on his coat behind.

Scrooge had often heard it said that Marley had no bowels, but he had never believed it until now.

No, nor did he believe it even now. Though he looked the phantom through and through, and saw it standing before him,—though he felt the chilling influence of its death-cold eyes, and noticed the very texture of the folded kerchief bound about its head and chin,—he was still incredulous.

"How now!" said Scrooge, caustic and cold as ever. "What do you want with me?"

"Much!"—Marley's voice, no doubt about it.

"Who are you?"

"Ask me who I *was*."

"Who *were* you then?"

"In life I was your partner, Jacob Marley."

"Can you—can you sit down?"

"I can."

"Do it, then."

Scrooge asked the question, because he didn't know whether a ghost so transparent might find himself in a condition to take a chair; and felt that, in the event of its being impossible, it might involve the necessity of an embarrassing explanation. But the ghost sat down on the opposite side of the fireplace, as if he were quite used to it.

"You don't believe in me."

"I don't."

"What evidence would you have of my reality beyond that of your senses?"

"I don't know."

"Why do you doubt your senses?"

"Because a little thing affects them. A slight disorder of the stomach makes them cheats. You may be an undigested bit of beef, a blot of mustard, a crumb of cheese, a fragment of an underdone potato. There's more of gravy than of grave about you, whatever you are!"

Scrooge was not much in the habit of cracking jokes, nor did he feel in his heart by any means waggish then. The truth is, that he tried to be smart, as a means of distracting his own attention, and keeping down his horror.

But how much greater was his horror when, the phantom taking off the bandage round its head, as if it were too warm to wear in-doors, its lower jaw dropped down upon its breast!

"Mercy! Dreadful apparition, why do you trouble me? Why do spirits walk the earth, and why do they come to me?"

"It is required of every man, that the spirit within him should walk abroad among his fellowmen, and travel far and wide; and if that spirit goes not forth in life, it is condemned to do so after death. I cannot tell you all I would. A very little more is permitted to me. I cannot rest, I cannot stay, I cannot linger anywhere. My spirit never walked beyond our counting-house—mark me!—in life my spirit never roved beyond the narrow limits of our money-changing hole; and weary journeys lie before me!"

"Seven years dead. And travelling all the time? You travel fast?"

"On the wings of the wind."

"You might have got over a great quantity of ground in seven years."

"O blind man, blind man! not to know that ages of incessant labor by immortal creatures for this earth must pass into eternity before the good of which it is susceptible is all developed. Not to know that any Christian spirit working kindly in its little sphere, whatever it may be, will find its mortal life too short for its vast means of usefulness. Not to know that no space of regret can make amends for one life's opportunities misused! Yet I was like this man; I once was like this man!"

"But you were always a good man of business, Jacob,"

faltered Scrooge, who now began to apply this to himself.

"Business!" cried the Ghost, wringing its hands again. "Mankind was my business. The common welfare was my business; charity, mercy, forbearance, benevolence, were all my business. The dealings of my trade were but a drop of water in the comprehensive ocean of my business!"

Scrooge was very much dismayed to hear the spectre going on at this rate, and began to quake exceedingly.

"Hear me! My time is nearly gone."

"I will. But don't be hard upon me! Don't be flowery, Jacob! Pray!"

"I am here to-night to warn you that you have yet a chance and hope of escaping my fate. A chance and hope of my procuring, Ebenezer."

"You were always a good friend to me. Thank'ee!"

"You will be haunted by Three Spirits."

"Is that the chance and hope you mentioned, Jacob? I—I think I'd rather not."

"Without their visits, you cannot hope to shun the path I tread. Expect the first to-morrow night, when the bell tolls One. Expect the second on the next night at the same hour. The third, upon the next night, when the last stroke of Twelve has ceased to vibrate. Look to see me no more; and look that, for your own sake, you remember what has passed between us!"

It walked backward from him; and at every step it took, the window raised itself a little, so that, when the apparition reached it, it was wide open.

Scrooge closed the window, and examined the door by which the Ghost had entered. It was double-locked, as he had locked it with his own hands, and the bolts were undisturbed. Scrooge tried to say, "Humbug!" but stopped at the first syllable. And being, from the emotion he had undergone, or the fatigues of the day, or his glimpse of the invisible world, or the dull conversation of the Ghost, or the lateness of the hour, much in need of repose, he went straight to bed, without undressing, and fell asleep on the instant.

THE FIRST OF THE THREE SPIRITS

When Scrooge awoke, it was so dark, that, looking out of bed, he could scarcely distinguish the transparent window from the opaque walls of his chamber, until suddenly the church clock tolled a deep, dull, hollow, melancholy ONE.

Light flashed up in the room upon the instant, and the curtains of his bed were drawn aside by a strange figure,—like a child: yet not so like a child as like an old man, viewed through some supernatural medium, which gave him the appearance of having receded from the view, and being diminished to a child's proportions. Its hair, which hung about its neck and down its back, was white as if with age; and yet the face had not a wrinkle in it, and the tenderest bloom was on the skin. It held a branch of fresh green holly in its hand; and, in singular contradiction of that wintry emblem, had its dress trimmed with summer flowers. But the strangest thing about it was, that from the crown of its head there sprung a bright clear jet of light, by which all this was visible; and which was doubtless the occasion of its using, in its duller moments, a great extinguisher for a cap, which it now held under its arm.

"Are you the Spirit, sir, whose coming was foretold to me?"

"I am!"

"Who and what are you?"

"I am the Ghost of Christmas Past."

"Long past?"

"No. Your past. The things that you will see with me are shadows of the things that have been; they will have no consciousness of us."

Scrooge then made bold to inquire what business brought him there.

"Your welfare. Rise, and walk with me!"

It would have been in vain for Scrooge to plead that the weather and the hour were not adapted to pedestrian purposes; that bed was warm, and the thermometer a long way below freezing; that he was clad but lightly in his slippers, dressing-gown, and nightcap; and that he had a cold upon him at that time. The grasp, though gentle as a woman's hand, was not to be resisted. He rose; but finding that the Spirit made towards the window, clasped its robe in supplication.

"I am a mortal, and liable to fall."

"Bear but a touch of my hand *there,*" said the Spirit, laying it upon his heart, "and you shall be upheld in more than this!"

As the words were spoken, they passed through the wall, and stood in the busy thoroughfares of a city. It was made plain enough by the dressing of the shops that here, too, it was Christmas time.

The Ghost stopped at a certain warehouse door, and asked Scrooge if he knew it.

"Know it! I Was apprenticed here!"

They went in. At sight of an old gentleman in a Welsh wig, sitting behind such a high desk that, if he had been two inches taller, he must have knocked his head against the ceiling, Scrooge cried in great excitement: "Why, it's old Fezziwig! Bless his heart, it's Fezziwig, alive again!"

Old Fezziwig laid down his pen, and looked up at the clock, which pointed to the hour of seven. He rubbed his hands; adjusted his capacious waistcoat; laughed all over himself, from his shoes to his organ of benevolence; and called out in a comfortable, oily, rich, fat, jovial voice: "Yo ho, there! Ebenezer! Dick!"

A living and moving picture of Scrooge's former self, a young man, came briskly in, accompanied by his fellow-prentice.

"Dick Wilkins, to be sure!" said Scrooge to the Ghost. "My old fellow-prentice, bless me, yes. There he is. He was very much attached to me, was Dick. Poor Dick! Dear, dear!"

"Yo ho, my boys!" said Fezziwig. "No more work tonight. Christmas eve, Dick. Christmas, Ebenezer! Let's have the shutters up, before a man can say Jack Robinson! Clear away, my lads, and let's have lots of room here!"

Clear away! There was nothing they wouldn't have cleared away, or couldn't have cleared away, with old Fezziwig looking on. It was done in a minute. Every movable was packed off, as if it were dismissed from public life forevermore; the floor was swept and watered, the lamps were trimmed, fuel was heaped upon the fire; and the warehouse was as snug and warm and dry and bright a ball-room as you would desire to see upon a winter's night.

In came a fiddler with a music-book, and went up to the lofty desk, and made an orchestra of it, and tuned like fifty stomach-aches. In came Mrs. Fezziwig, one vast substantial smile. In came the three Miss Fezziwigs, beaming and lovable. In came the six young followers whose hearts they broke. In came all the young men and women employed in the business. In came the housemaid, with her cousin the baker. In came the cook, with her brother's particular friend the milkman. In they all came one after another; some shyly, some boldly, some gracefully, some awkwardly, some pushing, some pulling; in they all came, anyhow and everyhow. Away they all went, twenty couples at once; hands half round and back again the other way; down the middle and up again; round and round in various stages of affectionate grouping; old top couple always turning up in the wrong place; new top couple starting off again, as soon as they got there; all top couples at last, and not a bottom one to help them. When this result was brought about, old Fezziwig, clapping his hands to stop the dance, cried out, "Well done!" and the fiddler plunged his hot face into a pot of porter especially provided for that purpose.

There were more dances, and there were forfeits, and more dances, and there was cake, and there was negus, and there was a great piece of Cold Roast, and there was a great piece of Cold Boiled, and there were mince-pies, and plenty of beer. But the great effect of the evening came after the

Roast and Boiled, when the fiddler struck up "Sir Roger de Coverley." Then old Fezziwig stood out to dance with Mrs. Fezziwig. Top couple, too; with a good stiff piece of work cut out for them; three or four and twenty pair of partners; people who were not to be trifled with; people who *would* dance, and had no notion of walking.

But if they had been twice as many,—four times,—old Fezziwig would have been a match for them, and so would Mrs. Fezziwig. As to *her,* she was worthy to be his partner in every sense of the term. A positive light appeared to issue from Fezziwig's calves. They shone in every part of the dance. You couldn't have predicted, at any given time, what would become of 'em next. And when old Fezziwig and Mrs. Fezziwig had gone all through the dance,—advance and retire, turn your partner, bow and courtesy, corkscrew, thread the needle, and back again to your place,—Fezziwig "cut,"—cut so deftly, that he appeared to wink with his legs.

When the clock struck eleven this domestic hall broke up. Mr. and Mrs. Fezziwig took their stations, one on either side the door, and, shaking hands with every person individually as he or she went out, wished him or her a Merry Christmas. When everybody had retired but the two 'prentices, they did the same to them; and thus the cheerful voices died away, and the lads were left to their beds, which were under a counter in the back shop.

"A small matter," said the Ghost, "to make these silly folks so full of gratitude. He has spent but a few pounds of your mortal money,—three or four perhaps. Is that so much that he deserves this praise?"

"It isn't that," said Scrooge, heated by the remark, and speaking unconsciously like his former, not his latter self,—"it isn't that, Spirit. He has the power to render us happy or unhappy; to make our service light or burdensome; a pleasure or a toil. Say that his power lies in words and looks; in things so slight and insignificant that it is impossible to add and count 'em up: what then? The happiness he gives is quite as

great as if it cost a fortune."

He felt the Spirit's glance, and stopped.

"What is the matter?"

"Nothing particular."

"Something, I think?"

"No, no. I should like to be able to say a word or two to my clerk just now. That's all."

"My time grows short," observed the Spirit. "Quick!"

This was not addressed to Scrooge, or to any one whom he could see, but it produced an immediate effect. For again he saw himself. He was older now; a man in the prime of life.

He was not alone, but sat by the side of a fair young girl in a black dress, in whose eyes there were tears.

"It matters little," she said softly to Scrooge's former self. "To you, very little. Another idol has displaced me; and if it can comfort you in time to come, as I would have tried to do, I have no just cause to grieve."

"What idol has displaced you?"

"A golden one. You fear the world too much. I have seen your nobler aspirations fall off one by one, until the master-passion, Gain, engrosses you. Have I not?"

"What then? Even if I have grown so much wiser, what

then? I am not changed towards you. Have I ever sought release from our engagement?"

"In words, no. Never."

"In what, then?"

"In a changed nature; in an altered spirit; in another atmosphere of life; another Hope as its great end. If you were free to-day, to-morrow, yesterday, can even I believe that you would choose a dowerless girl; or, choosing her, do I not know that your repentance and regret would surely follow? I do; and I release you. With a full heart, for the love of him you once were."

"Spirit! remove me from this place."

"I told you these were shadows of the things that have been," said the Ghost. "That they are what they are, do not blame me!"

"Remove me!" Scrooge exclaimed. "I cannot bear it! Leave me! Take me back. Haunt me no longer!"

As he struggled with the Spirit he was conscious of being exhausted, and overcome by an irresistible drowsiness; and, further, of being in his own bedroom. He had barely time to reel to bed before he sank into a heavy sleep.

THE SECOND OF THE THREE SPIRITS

Scrooge awoke in his own bedroom. There was no doubt about that. But it and his own adjoining sitting-room, into which he shuffled in his slippers, attracted by a great light there, had undergone a surprising transformation. The walls and ceiling were so hung with living green, that it looked a perfect grove. The leaves of holly, mistletoe, and ivy reflected back the light, as if so many little mirrors had been scattered there; and such a mighty blaze went roaring up the chimney, as that petrifaction of a hearth had never known in Scrooge's time, or Marley's, or for many and many a winter season gone. Heaped upon the floor, to form a kind of throne, were turkeys, geese, game, brawn, great joints of meat, sucking pigs, long wreaths of sausages, mince-pies, plum-puddings, barrels of oysters, red-hot chestnuts, cherry-cheeked apples, juicy oranges, luscious pears, immense twelfth-cakes, and great bowls of punch. In easy state upon this couch there sat a Giant glorious to see; who bore a glowing torch, in shape not unlike Plenty's horn, and who raised it high to shed its light on Scrooge, as he came peeping round the door.

"Come in,—come in! and know me better, man! I am the Ghost of Christmas Present. Look upon me! You have never seen the like of me before!"

"Never."

"Have never walked forth with the younger members of

my family; meaning (for I am very young) my elder brothers born in these later years?" pursued the Phantom.

"I don't think I have, I am afraid I have not. Have you had many brothers, Spirit?"

"More than eighteen hundred."

"A tremendous family to provide for! Spirit, conduct me where you will. I went forth last night on compulsion, and I learnt a lesson which is working now. To-night, if you have aught to teach me, let me profit by it."

"Touch my robe!"

Scrooge did as he was told, and held it fast.

The room and its contents all vanished instantly, and they stood in the city streets upon a snowy Christmas morning.

Scrooge and the Ghost passed on, invisible, straight to Scrooge's clerk's; and on the threshold of the door the Spirit smiled, and stopped to bless Bob Cratchit's dwelling with the sprinklings of his torch. Think of that! Bob had but fifteen "bob" a week himself; he pocketed on Saturdays but fifteen copies of his Christian name; and yet the Ghost of Christmas Present blessed his four-roomed house!

Then up rose Mrs. Cratchit, Cratchit's wife, dressed out but poorly in a twice-turned gown, but brave in ribbons, which are cheap and make a goodly show for sixpence; and she laid the cloth, assisted by Belinda Cratchit, second of her daughters, also brave in ribbons; while Master Peter Cratchit plunged a fork into the saucepan of potatoes, and, getting the corners of his monstrous shirt-collar (Bob's private property, conferred upon his son and heir in honor of the day) into his mouth, rejoiced to find himself so gallantly attired, and yearned to show his linen in the fashionable Parks. And now two smaller Cratchits, boy and girl came tearing in, screaming that outside the baker's they had smelt the goose, and known it for their own; and, basking in luxurious thoughts of sage and onion, these young Cratchits danced about the table, and exalted Master Peter Cratchit to the skies, while he (not proud, although his collars nearly choked him) blew the fire, until the slow potatoes, bubbling up, knocked loudly at the saucepan-lid to be let out and peeled.

"What has ever got your precious father then?" said Mrs. Cratchit. "And your brother Tiny Tim! And Martha warn't as late last Christmas day by half an hour!"

"Here's Martha, mother!" said a girl, appearing as she spoke.

"Here's Martha, mother!" cried the two young Cratchits. "Hurrah! There's *such* a goose, Martha!"

"Why, bless your heart alive, my dear, how late you are!" said Mrs. Cratchit, kissing her a dozen times, and taking off her shawl and bonnet for her.

"We'd a deal of work to finish up last night," replied the girl, "and had to clear away this morning, mother!"

"Well! Never mind so long as you are come," said Mrs. Cratchit. "Sit ye down before the fire, my dear, and have a warm, Lord bless ye!"

"No, no! There's father coming," cried the two young Cratchits, who were everywhere at once. "Hide, Martha, hide!"

So Martha hid herself, and in came little Bob, the father, with at least three feet of comforter, exclusive of the fringe,

hanging down before him; and his threadbare clothes darned up and brushed, to look seasonable; and Tiny Tim upon his shoulder. Alas for Tiny Tim, he bore a little crutch, and had his limbs supported by an iron frame!

"Why, where's our Martha?" cried Bob Cratchit, looking round.

"Not coming," said Mrs. Cratchit.

"Not coming!" said Bob, with a sudden declension in his high spirits; for he had been Tim's blood-horse all the way from church, and had come home rampant,—"not coming upon Christmas day!"

Martha didn't like to see him disappointed, if it were only in joke; so she came out prematurely from behind the closet door, and ran into his arms, while the two young Cratchits hustled Tiny Tim, and bore him off into the wash-house, that he might hear the pudding singing in the copper.

"And how did little Tim behave?" asked Mrs. Cratchit, when she had rallied Bob on his credulity, and Bob had hugged his daughter to his heart's content.

"As good as gold," said Bob, "and better. Somehow he gets thoughtful, sitting by himself so much, and thinks the strangest things you ever heard. He told me, coming home, that he hoped the people saw him in the church, because he was a cripple, and it might be pleasant to them to remember, upon Christmas day, who made lame beggars walk and blind men see."

Bob's voice was tremulous when he told them this, and trembled more when he said that Tiny Tim was growing strong and hearty.

His active little crutch was heard upon the floor, and back came Tiny Tim before another word was spoken, escorted by his brother and sister to his stool beside the fire; and while Bob, turning up his cuffs,—as if, poor fellow, they were capable of being made more shabby,—compounded some hot mixture in a jug with gin and lemons, and stirred it round and round and put it on the hob to simmer, Master Peter and the two ubiquitous young Cratchits went to fetch the goose, with which they soon returned in high procession.

Mrs. Cratchit made the gravy (ready beforehand in a little saucepan) hissing hot; Master Peter mashed the potatoes with incredible vigor; Miss Belinda sweetened up the apple-sauce; Martha dusted the hot plates; Bob took Tiny Tim beside him in a tiny corner at the table; the two young Cratchits set chairs for everybody, not forgetting themselves, and mounting guard upon their posts, crammed spoons into their mouths, lest they should shriek for goose before their turn came to be helped. At last the dishes were set on, and grace was said. It was succeeded by a breathless pause, as Mrs. Cratchit, looking slowly all along the carving-knife, prepared to plunge it in the breast; but when she did, and when the long-expected gush of stuffing issued forth, one murmur of delight arose all round the board, and even Tiny Tim, excited by the two young Cratchits, beat on the table with the handle of his knife, and feebly cried, Hurrah!

There never was such a goose. Bob said he didn't believe there ever was such a goose cooked. Its tenderness and flavor, size and cheapness, were the themes of universal admiration. Eked out by apple-sauce and mashed potatoes, it was a sufficient dinner for the whole family; indeed, as Mrs. Cratchit said with great delight (surveying one small atom of a bone upon the dish), they hadn't ate it all at last! Yet every one had had enough, and the youngest Cratchits in particular were steeped in sage and onion to the eyebrows! But now, the plates being changed by Miss Belinda, Mrs. Cratchit left the room alone,—too nervous to bear witnesses,—to take the pudding up, and bring it in.

Suppose it should not be done enough! Suppose it should break in turning out! Suppose somebody should have got over the wall of the back yard, and stolen it, while they were merry with the goose,—a supposition at which the two young Cratchits became livid! All sorts of horrors were supposed.

Hallo! A great deal of steam! The pudding was out of the copper. A smell like a washing-day! That was the cloth. A smell like an eating-house and a pastry-cook's next door to each other, with a laundress's next door to that! That was the pudding! In half a minute Mrs. Cratchit entered,—flushed but smiling proudly,—with the pudding, like a speckled cannon-ball, so hard and firm, blazing in half of half a quartern of ignited brandy, and bedight with Christmas holly stuck into the top.

O, a wonderful pudding! Bob Cratchit said, and calmly too, that he regarded it as the greatest success achieved by Mrs. Cratchit since their marriage. Mrs. Cratchit said that now the weight was off her mind, she would confess she had had her doubts about the quantity of flour. Everybody had something to say about it, but nobody said or thought it was at all a small pudding for a large family. Any Cratchit would have blushed to hint at such a thing.

At last the dinner was all done, the cloth was cleared, the hearth swept, and the fire made up. The compound in the jug being tasted, and considered perfect, apples and oranges were

put upon the table, and a shovelful of chestnuts on the fire.

Then all the Cratchit family drew round the hearth, in what Bob Cratchit called a circle, and at Bob Cratchit's elbow stood the family display of glass,—two tumblers, and a custard-cup without a handle.

These held the hot stuff from the jug, however, as well as golden goblets would have done; and Bob served it out with beaming looks, while the chestnuts on the fire sputtered and crackled noisily. Then Bob proposed:—

"A Merry Christmas to us all, my dears. God bless us!"

Which all the family re-echoed.

"God bless us every one!" said Tiny Tim, the last of all.

He sat very close to his father's side, upon his little stool. Bob held his withered little hand in his, as if he loved the child, and wished to keep him by his side, and dreaded that he might be taken from him.

Scrooge raised his head speedily, on hearing his own name.

"Mr. Scrooge!" said Bob; "I'll give you Mr. Scrooge, the Founder of the Feast!"

"The Founder of the Feast indeed!" cried Mrs. Cratchit, reddening. "I wish I had him here. I'd give him a piece of my mind to feast upon, and I hope he'd have a good appetite for it."

"My dear," said Bob, "the children! Christmas day."

"It should be Christmas day, I am sure," said she, "on which one drinks the health of such an odious, stingy, hard, unfeeling man as Mr. Scrooge. You know he is, Robert! Nobody knows it better than you do, poor fellow!"

"My dear," was Bob's mild answer, "Christmas day."

"I'll drink his health for your sake and the day's," said Mrs. Cratchit, "not for his. Long life to him! A merry Christmas and a happy New Year! He'll be very merry and very happy, I have no doubt!"

The children drank the toast after her. It was the first of their proceedings which had no heartiness in it. Tiny Tim drank it last of all, but he didn't care twopence for it. Scrooge was the Ogre of the family. The mention of his name cast a dark shadow on the party, which was not dispelled for full five minutes.

After it had passed away, they were ten times merrier than before, from the mere relief of Scrooge the Baleful being done with. Bob Cratchit told them how he had a situation in his eye for Master Peter, which would bring in, if obtained, full five and sixpence weekly. The two young Cratchits laughed tremendously at the idea of Peter's being a man of business; and Peter himself looked thoughtfully at the fire from between his collars, as if he were deliberating what particular investments he should favor when he came into the receipt of that bewildering income. Martha, who was a poor apprentice at a milliner's, then told them what kind of work she had to do, and how many hours she worked at a stretch, and how she meant to lie abed to-morrow morning for a good long rest; to-morrow being a holiday she passed at home. Also how she had seen a countess and a lord some days before, and how the lord "was much about as tall as Peter"; at which Peter pulled up his collars so high that you couldn't have seen his head if you had been there. All this time the chestnuts and the jug went round and round; and by and by they had a song, about a lost child travelling in the snow, from Tiny Tim, who had a plaintive little voice, and sang it very well indeed.

There was nothing of high mark in this. They were not a handsome family; they were not well dressed; their shoes were far from being water-proof; their clothes were scanty; and Peter might have known, and very likely did, the inside of a pawn-broker's. But they were happy, grateful, pleased with one another, and contented with the time; and when they faded, and looked happier yet in the bright sprinklings of the Spirit's torch at parting, Scrooge had his eye upon them, and especially on Tiny Tim, until the last.

It was a great surprise to Scrooge, as this scene vanished, to hear a hearty laugh. It was a much greater surprise to Scrooge to recognize it as his own nephew's, and to find himself in a bright, dry, gleaming room, with the Spirit standing smiling by his side, and looking at that same nephew.

It is a fair, even-handed, noble adjustment of things, that while there is infection in disease and sorrow, there is nothing in the world so irresistibly contagious as laughter and good-humor. When Scrooge's nephew laughed, Scrooge's niece by marriage laughed as heartily as he. And their assembled friends, being not a bit behindhand, laughed out lustily.

"He said that Christmas was a humbug, as I live!" cried Scrooge's nephew. "He believed it too!"

"More shame for him, Fred!" said Scrooge's niece, indignantly. Bless those women! they never do anything by halves. They are always in earnest.

She was very pretty; exceedingly pretty. With a dimpled, surprised-looking, capital face; a ripe little mouth that seemed made to be kissed,—as no doubt it was; all kinds of good little dots about her chin, that melted into one another when she laughed; and the sunniest pair of eyes you ever saw in any little creature's head. Altogether she was what you would have called provoking, but satisfactory, too. O, perfectly satisfactory.

"He's a comical old fellow," said Scrooge's nephew, "that's the truth; and not so pleasant as he might be. However, his offences carry their own punishment, and I have nothing to say against him. Who suffers by his ill whims? Himself, always. Here he takes it into his head to dislike us, and he won't come and dine with us. What's the consequence? He don't lose much of a dinner."

"Indeed, I think he loses a very good dinner," interrupted Scrooge's niece. Everybody else said the same, and they must be allowed to have been competent judges, because they had just had dinner; and, with the dessert upon the table, were clustered round the fire, by lamplight.

"Well, I am very glad to hear it," said Scrooge's nephew, "because I haven't any great faith in these young housekeepers. What do *you* say, Topper?"

Topper clearly had his eye on one of Scrooge's niece's sisters, for he answered that a bachelor was a wretched outcast, who had no right to express an opinion on the subject. Whereat Scrooge's niece's sister—the plump one with the lace tucker; not the one with the roses—blushed.

After tea they had some music. For they were a musical family, and knew what they were about, when they sung a Glee or Catch, I can assure you,—especially Topper, who could growl away in the bass like a good one, and never swell the large veins in his forehead, or get red in the face over it.

But they didn't devote the whole evening to music. After a while they played at forfeits; for it is good to be children sometimes, and never better than at Christmas, when its mighty Founder was a child himself. There was first a game at blind man's-buff though. And I no more believe Topper was really blinded than I believe he had eyes in his boots. Because the way in which he went after that plump sister in the lace tucker was an outrage on the credulity of human nature. Knocking down the fire-irons, tumbling over the chairs, bumping up against the piano, smothering himself among the curtains, wherever she went there went he! He always knew where

the plump sister was. He wouldn't catch anybody else. If you had fallen up against him, as some of them did, and stood there, he would have made a feint of endeavoring to seize you, which would have been an affront to your understanding, and would instantly have sidled off in the direction of the plump sister.

"Here is a new game," said Scrooge. "One half-hour, Spirit, only one!"

It was a Game called Yes and No, where Scrooge's nephew had to think of something, and the rest must find out what; he only answering to their questions yes or no, as the case was. The fire of questioning to which he was exposed elicited from him that he was thinking of an animal, a live animal, rather a disagreeable animal, a savage animal, an animal that growled and grunted sometimes, and talked sometimes, and lived in London, and walked about the streets, and wasn't made a show of, and wasn't led by anybody, and didn't live in a menagerie, and was never killed in a market, and was not a horse, or an ass, or a cow, or a bull, or a tiger, or a dog, or a pig, or a cat, or a bear. At every new question put to him, this nephew burst into a fresh roar of laughter; and was so inexpressibly tickled, that he was obliged to get up off the sofa and stamp. At last the plump sister cried out:—

"I have found it out! I know what it is, Fred! I know what it is!"

"What is it?" cried Fred.

"It's your uncle Scro-o-o-o-oge!"

Which it certainly was. Admiration was the universal sentiment, though some objected that the reply to "Is it a bear?" ought to have been "Yes."

Uncle Scrooge had imperceptibly become so gay and light of heart, that he would have drank to the unconscious company in an inaudible speech. But the whole scene passed off in the breath of the last word spoken by his nephew; and he and the Spirit were again upon their travels.

Much they saw, and far they went, and many homes they visited, but always with a happy end. The Spirit stood beside sick-beds, and they were cheerful; on foreign lands, and they were close at home; by struggling men, and they were patient in their greater hope; by poverty, and it was rich. In almshouse, hospital, and jail, in misery's every refuge, where vain man in his little brief authority had not made fast the door, and barred the Spirit out, he left his blessing, and taught Scrooge his precepts. Suddenly, as they stood together in an open place, the bell struck twelve.

Scrooge looked about him for the Ghost, and saw it no more. As the last stroke ceased to vibrate, he remembered the prediction of old Jacob Marley, and, lifting up his eyes, beheld a solemn Phantom, draped and hooded, coming like a mist along the ground towards him.

THE LAST OF THE SPIRITS

The Phantom slowly, gravely, silently approached. When it came near him, Scrooge bent down upon his knee; for in the air through which this Spirit moved it seemed to scatter gloom and mystery.

It was shrouded in a deep black garment, which concealed its head, its face, its form, and left nothing of it visible save one outstretched hand. He knew no more, for the Spirit neither spoke nor moved.

"I am in the presence of the Ghost of Christmas Yet To Come? Ghost of the Future! I fear you more than any spectre I have seen. But as I know your purpose is to do me good, and as I hope to live to be another man from what I was, I am prepared to bear you company, and do it with a thankful heart. Will you not speak to me?"

It gave him no reply. The hand was pointed straight before them.

"Lead on! Lead on! The night is waning fast, and it is precious time to me, I know. Lead on, Spirit!"

They scarcely seemed to enter the city; for the city rather seemed to spring up about them. But there they were in the heart of it; on 'Change, amongst the merchants.

The Spirit stopped beside one little knot of business men. Observing that the hand was pointed to them, Scrooge advanced to listen to their talk.

"No," said a great fat man with a monstrous chin, "I don't know much about it either way. I only know he's dead."

"When did he die?" inquired another.

"Last night, I believe."

"Why, what was the matter with him? I thought he'd never die."

"God knows," said the first, with a yawn.

"What has he done with his money?" asked a red-faced gentleman.

"I haven't heard," said the man with the large chin. "Company, perhaps. He hasn't left it to me. That's all I know. By, by!"

Scrooge was at first inclined to be surprised that the Spirit should attach importance to conversation apparently so

trivial; but feeling assured that it must have some hidden purpose, he set himself to consider what it was likely to be. It could scarcely be supposed to have any bearing on the death of Jacob, his old partner, for that was Past, and this Ghost's province was the Future.

He looked about in that very place for his own image; but another man stood in his accustomed corner, and though the clock pointed to his usual time of day for being there, he saw no likeness of himself among the multitudes that poured in through the Porch. It gave him little surprise, however; for he had been revolving in his mind a change of life, and he thought and hoped he saw his new-born resolutions carried out in this.

They left this busy scene, and went into an obscure part of the town, to a low shop where iron, old rags, bottles, bones, and greasy offal were bought. A gray-haired rascal, of great age, sat smoking his pipe.

Scrooge and the Phantom came into the presence of this man, just as a woman with a heavy bundle slunk into the shop. But she had scarcely entered, when another woman, similarly laden, came in too; and she was closely followed by a man in faded black. After a short period of blank astonishment, in which the old man with the pipe had joined them, they all three burst into a laugh.

"Let the charwoman alone to be the first!" cried she who had entered first. "Let the laundress alone to be the second; and let the undertaker's man alone to be the third. Look here, old Joe, here's a chance! If we haven't all three met here without meaning it!"

"You couldn't have met in a better place. You were made free of it long ago, you know; and the other two ain't strangers. What have you got to sell? What have you got to sell?"

"Half a minute's patience, Joe, and you shall see."

"What odds then! What odds, Mrs. Dilber?" said the woman. "Every person has a right to take care of themselves. *He* always did! Who's the worse for the loss of a few things like these? Not a dead man, I suppose."

Mrs. Dilber, whose manner was remarkable for general propitiation, said, "No, indeed, ma'am."

"If he wanted to keep 'em after he was dead, a wicked old screw, why wasn't he natural in his life-time? If he had been, he'd have had somebody to look after him when he was struck with Death, instead of lying gasping out his last there, alone by himself."

"It's the truest word that ever was spoke, it's a judgment on him."

"I wish it was a little heavier judgment, and it should have been, you may depend upon it, if I could have laid my hands on anything else. Open that bundle, old Joe, and let me know the value of it. Speak out plain. I'm not afraid to be the first, nor afraid for them to see it."

Joe went down on his knees for the greater convenience of opening the bundle, and dragged out a large and heavy roll of some dark stuff.

"What do you call this? Bed-curtains!"

"Ah! Bed-curtains! Don't drop that oil upon the blankets, now."

"*His* blankets?"

"Whose else's do you think? He isn't likely to take cold without 'em, I dare say. Ah! You may look through that shirt till your eyes ache; but you won't find a hole in it, nor a thread

bare place. It's the best he had, and a fine one too. They'd have wasted it by dressing him up in it, if it hadn't been for me."

Scrooge listened to this dialogue in horror.

"Spirit! I see, I see. The case of this unhappy man might be my own. My life tends that way, now. Merciful Heaven, what is this!"

The scene had changed, and now he almost touched a bare, uncurtained bed. A pale light, rising in the outer air, fell straight upon this bed; and on it, unwatched, unwept, uncared for, was the body of this plundered unknown man.

"Spirit, let me see some tenderness connected with a death, or this dark chamber, Spirit, will be forever present to me."

The Ghost conducted him to poor Bob Cratchit's house,—the dwelling he had visited before,—and found the mother and the children seated round the fire.

Quiet. Very quiet. The noisy little Cratchits were as still as statues in one corner, and sat looking up at Peter, who had a book before him. The mother and her daughters were engaged in needle-work. But surely they were very quiet!

" 'And he took a child, and set him in the midst of them.' "

Where had Scrooge heard those words? He had not dreamed them. The boy must have read them out, as he and the Spirit crossed the threshold. Why did he not go on?

The mother laid her work upon the table, and put her hand up to her face.

"The color hurts my eyes," she said.

The color? Ah, poor Tiny Tim!

"They're better now again. It makes them weak by candle-light; and I wouldn't show weak eyes to your father when he comes home, for the world. It must be near his time."

"Past it rather," Peter answered, shutting up his book. "But I think he has walked a little slower than he used, these few last evenings, mother."

"I have known him walk with—I have known him walk

with Tiny Tim upon his shoulder, very fast indeed."

"And so have I," cried Peter. "Often."

"And so have I," exclaimed another. So had all.

"But he was very light to carry, and his father loved him so, that it was no trouble,—no trouble. And there is your father at the door!"

She hurried out to meet him; and little Bob in his comforter—he had need of it, poor fellow—came in. His tea was ready for him on the hob, and they all tried who should help him to it most. Then the two young Cratchits got upon his knees and laid, each child, a little cheek against his face, as if they said, "Don't mind it, father. Don't be grieved!"

Bob was very cheerful with them, and spoke pleasantly to all the family. He looked at the work upon the table, and praised the industry and speed of Mrs. Cratchit and the girls. They would be done long before Sunday, he said.

"Sunday! You went to-day, then, Robert?"

"Yes, my dear," returned Bob. "I wish you could have gone. It would have done you good to see how green a place it is. But you'll see it often. I promised him that I would walk there on a Sunday. My little, little child! My little child!"

He broke down all at once. He couldn't help it. If he could have helped it, he and his child would have been farther apart, perhaps, than they were.

"Spectre," said Scrooge, "something informs me that our parting moment is at hand. I know it, but I know not how. Tell me what man that was, with the covered face, whom we saw lying dead?"

The Ghost of Christmas Yet To Come conveyed him to a dismal, wretched, ruinous churchyard.

The Spirit stood among the graves, and pointed down to one.

"Before I draw nearer to that stone to which you point, answer me one question. Are these the shadows of the things that Will be, or are they shadows of the things that May be only?"

Still the Ghost pointed downward to the grave by which it stood.

"Men's courses will foreshadow certain ends, to which, if persevered in, they must lead. But if the courses be departed from, the ends will change. Say it is thus with what you show me!"

The Spirit was immovable as ever.

Scrooge crept towards it, trembling as he went; and, following the finger, read upon the stone of the neglected grave his own name,—EBENEZER SCROOGE.

"Am *I* that man who lay upon the bed? No, Spirit! O no, no! Spirit! hear me! I am not the man I was. I will not be the man I must have been but for this intercourse. Why show me this, if I am past all hope? Assure me that I yet may change these shadows you have shown me by an altered life."

For the first time the kind hand faltered.

"I will honor Christmas in my heart, and try to keep it all the year. I will live in the Past, the Present, and the Future. The Spirits of all three shall strive within me. I will not shut out the lessons that they teach. O, tell me I may sponge away the writing on this stone!"

Holding up his hands in one last prayer to have his fate reversed, he saw an alteration in the Phantom's hood and dress. It shrunk, collapsed, and dwindled down into a bedpost.

Yes, and the bedpost was his own. The bed was his own, the room was his own. Best and happiest of all, the Time before him was his own, to make amends in!

He was checked in his transports by the churches ringing out the lustiest peals he had ever heard.

Running to the window, he opened it, and put out his head. No fog, no mist, no night; clear, bright, stirring, golden day.

"What's to-day?" cried Scrooge, calling downward to a boy in Sunday clothes, who perhaps had loitered in to look about him.

"EH?"

"What's to-day, my fine fellow?"

"To-day! Why, CHRISTMAS DAY."

"It's Christmas day! I haven't missed it. Hallo, my fine fellow!"

"Hallo!"

"Do you know the Poulterer's, in the next street but one, at the corner?"

"I should hope I did."

"An intelligent boy! A remarkable boy! Do you know whether they've sold the prize Turkey that was hanging up there? Not the little prize Turkey,—the big one?"

"What, the one as big as me?"

"What a delightful boy! It's a pleasure to talk to him. Yes, my buck!"

"It's hanging there now."

"Is it? Go and buy it."

"Walk-ER!" exclaimed the boy.

"No, no, I am in earnest. Go and buy it, and tell 'em to bring it here, that I may give them the direction where to take it. Come back with the man, and I'll give you a shilling. Come back with him in less than five minutes, and I'll give you half a crown!"

The boy was off like a shot.

"I'll send it to Bob Cratchit's! He sha'n't know who sends it. It's twice the size of Tiny Tim. Joe Miller never made such a joke as sending it to Bob's will be!"

The hand in which he wrote the address was not a steady one; but write it he did, somehow, and went down stairs to open the street door, ready for the coming of the poulterer's man.

It *was* a Turkey! He never could have stood upon his legs, that bird. He would have snapped 'em short off in a minute, like sticks of sealing-wax.

Scrooge dressed himself "all in his best," and at last got out into the streets. The people were by this time pouring forth, as he had seen them with the Ghost of Christmas Present; and, walking with his hands behind him, Scrooge regarded every one with a delighted smile. He looked so irresistibly pleasant, in a word, that three or four good-humored fellows said, "Good morning, sir! A merry Christmas to you!" And Scrooge said often afterwards, that, of all the blithe sounds he had ever heard, those were the blithest in his ears.

In the afternoon, he turned his steps towards his nephew's house.

He passed the door a dozen times, before he had the courage to go up and knock. But he made a dash, and did it.

"Is your master at home, my dear?" said Scrooge to the girl. Nice girl! Very.

"Yes, sir."

"Where is he, my love?"

"He's in the dining-room, sir, along with mistress."

"He knows me," said Scrooge, with his hand already on the dining-room lock. "I'll go in here, my dear."

"Fred!"

"Why, bless my soul!" cried Fred, "who's that?"

"It's I. Your uncle Scrooge. I have come to dinner. Will you let me in, Fred?"

Let him in! It is a mercy he didn't shake his arm off. He was at home in five minutes. Nothing could be heartier. His niece looked just the same. So did Topper when *he* came. So did the plump sister, when *she* came. So did every one when *they* came. Wonderful party, wonderful games, wonderful unanimity, won-der-ful happiness!

But he was early at the office next morning. O, he was early there. If he could only be there first, and catch Bob Cratchit coming late! That was the thing he had set his heart upon.

And he did it. The clock struck nine. No Bob. A quarter past. No Bob. Bob was full eighteen minutes and a half behind his time. Scrooge sat with his door wide open, that he might see him come into the tank.

Bob's hat was off, before he opened the door; his comforter too. He was on his stool in a jiffy; driving away with his pen, as if he were trying to overtake nine o'clock.

"Hallo!" growled Scrooge, in his accustomed voice, as near as he could feign it. "What do you mean by coming here at this time of day?"

"I am very sorry, sir. I *am* behind my time."

"You are? Yes. I think you are. Step this way, if you please."

"It's only once a year, sir. It shall not be repeated. I was making rather merry yesterday, sir."

"Now, I'll tell you what, my friend. I am not going to stand this sort of thing any longer. And therefore," Scrooge continued, leaping from his stool, and giving Bob such a dig in the waist coat that he staggered back into the tank again,—"and therefore I am about to raise your salary!"

Bob trembled, and got a little nearer to the ruler.

"A merry Christmas, Bob!" said Scrooge, with an earnestness that could not be mistaken, as he clapped him on the back. "A merrier Christmas, Bob, my good fellow, than I have given you for many a year! I'll raise your salary, and endeavor to assist your struggling family, and we will discuss your affairs this very afternoon, over a Christmas bowl of smoking bishop, Bob! Make up the fires, and buy a second coal-scuttle before you dot another i, Bob Cratchit!"

Scrooge was better than his word. He did it all, and infinitely more; and to Tiny Tim, who did NOT die, he was a second father. He became as good a friend, as good a master, and as good a man as the good old city knew, or any other good old city, town, or borough in the good old world. Some people laughed to see the alteration in him; but his own heart laughed, and that was quite enough for him.

He had no further intercourse with Spirits, but lived in that respect upon the Total-Abstinence Principle ever afterwards; and it was always said of him, that he knew how to keep Christmas well, if any man alive possessed the knowledge. May that be truly said of us, and all of us! And so, as Tiny Tim observed, God Bless Us, Every One!

WISE SAYINGS FROM POOR RICHARD

From Poor Richard's Almanac

Every year, for almost twenty-five years, one of colonial America's favorite almanacs was Poor Richard's. In addition to the usual sundry bits of calendar information, weather forecasts and diverse notes on astrological and other odd subjects, it contained a treasury of wise sayings and witticisms. Poor Richard was really the pen-name of Benjamin Franklin, and the selections that follow are from the almanacs which Benjamin Franklin wrote and compiled more than two hundred years ago.

Light purse, heavy heart.

Hunger never saw bad bread.

Great talkers, little doers.

To lengthen thy life, lessen thy meals.

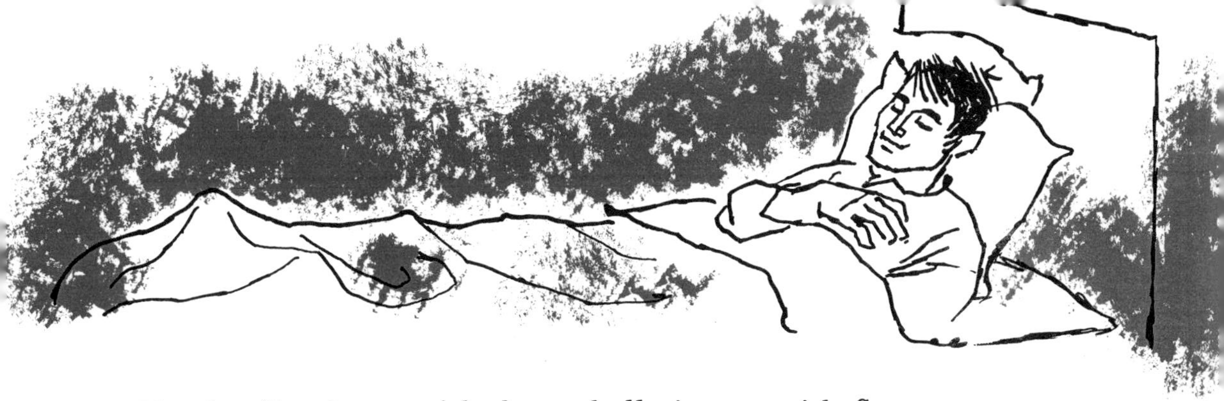

He that lies down with dogs, shall rise up with fleas.

Without justice courage is weak.

Many dishes, many diseases.

Teach your child to hold his tongue, he'll learn fast enough to speak.

He that cannot obey, cannot command.

An egg today is better than a hen tomorrow.

He that waits upon fortune, is never sure of a dinner.

A learned blockhead is a greater blockhead than an ignorant one.

Look before, or you'll find yourself behind.

Early to bed and early to rise,

makes a man healthy, wealthy, and wise.

Don't throw stones
at your neighbors,
if your own windows
are glass.

Well done is better than well said.

He that falls in
love with himself,
will have no rivals.

The noblest question in the world is, *What good may I do in it?*

Diligence is the
mother of good-luck.

An empty bag
cannot stand upright.

Observe all men;
thyself most.

Wish not so much
to live long as to live well.

Since thou art not sure of a minute, throw not away an hour.

He that speaks much, is much mistaken.

Wink at small faults; remember thou hast great ones.

Blessed is he that expects nothing, for he shall never be disappointed.

Tricks and treachery are the practice of fools, that have not wit enough to be honest.

They who have nothing
to be troubled at,
will be troubled
at nothing.

Tongue double, brings trouble.

A lie stands on one leg, truth on two.

Fools make feasts, and wise men eat 'em.

'Tis easier to prevent
bad habits than
to break them.

Learn of the skilful:

he that teaches himself,

hath a fool for his master.

If you would keep your secret from an enemy, tell it not to a friend.

Speak and speed: the close mouth catches no flies.

Experience keeps a dear school, yet fools will learn in no other.

The same man cannot be both friend and flatterer.

Beware of little expenses, a small leak will sink a great ship.

No gains without pains.

THE QUANGLE WANGLE'S HAT

I

On the top of the Crumpetty Tree
  The Quangle Wangle sat,
But his face you could not see,
  On account of his Beaver Hat.
For his Hat was a hundred and two feet wide,
With ribbons and bibbons on every side,
And bells, and buttons, and loops, and lace,
So that nobody ever could see the face
    Of the Quangle Wangle Quee.

II

The Quangle Wangle said
  To himself on the Crumpetty Tree,
  "Jam, and jelly, and bread
  Are the best of food for me!

But the longer I live on this Crumpetty Tree
The plainer than ever it seems to me
That very few people come this way
And that life on the whole is far from gay!"
Said the Quangle Wangle Quee.

III

But there came to the Crumpetty Tree
Mr. and Mrs. Canary;
And they said, "Did ever you see
Any spot so charmingly airy?
May we build a nest on your lovely Hat?
Mr. Quangle Wangle, grant us that!
O please let us come and build a nest
Of whatever material suits you best,
Mr. Quangle Wangle Quee!"

V

And the Golden Grouse came there,
  And the Pobble who has no toes,
And the small Olympian bear,
  And the Dong with a luminous nose.
And the Blue Baboon who played the flute,
And the Orient Calf from the Land of Tute,
And the Attery Squash, and the Bisky Bat,—
All came and built on the lovely Hat
    Of the Quangle Wangle Quee.

IV

And besides, to the Crumpetty Tree
  Came the Stork, the Duck, and the Owl;
The Snail and the Bumble-Bee,
  The Frog and the Fimble Fowl
(The Fimble Fowl, with a Corkscrew leg);
And all of them said, "We humbly beg
We may build our homes on your lovely Hat,—
Mr. Quangle Wangle, grant us that!
    Mr. Quangle Wangle Quee!"

VI

And the Quangle Wangle said
  To himself on the Crumpetty Tree,
"When all these creatures move
  What a wonderful noise there'll be!"
And at night by the light of the Mulberry moon
They danced to the Flute of the Blue Baboon,
On the broad green leaves of the Crumpetty Tree,
And all were as happy as happy could be,
    With the Quangle Wangle Quee.

Edward Lear

RASP
JA
L.L.B

THE SORCERER'S APPRENTICE

By Richard Rostron

MANY YEARS AGO, in far-off Switzerland, there lived a sorcerer. That is, this story took place many years ago. For all we know, the sorcerer may be living yet. His name then was Willibald, which is a little odd, but no stranger than he was. He was tall and thin, and his nose was long and pointed to match. He wore long, loose, trailing gowns. What was left of his hair was white. A small black cap sat on the back of his head.

He was not a very ordinary sorcerer. For instance, his fellow sorcerers specialized in disappearing in puffs of smoke. Then they would bob up, at a moment's notice, in places far away from where they had been a second before. But Willibald felt such tricks were beneath his dignity. To him they were a trifle show-offy. *He* traveled from place to place on a donkey. Of course, this took a good deal more time. But no one knew better than he did that he was no ordinary sorcerer, and that his customers would wait.

However, he did have a weakness for service. It was his habit to command pieces of furniture—chairs, tables, footstools, even brooms—to do his bidding. Of course, once in a while a passerby would be frightened out of his wits to see a table capering along the street with a bucket of water on its top. But this didn't happen often. The sorcerer lived 'way on the edge of town on a street that wasn't at all fashionable.

And he was usually very careful not to let anyone see him work his spells. Not even Fritzl, his apprentice, knew how it was done.

Fritzl was a boy who was learning the sorcery business. He wasn't very bright or industrious. He made mistakes, spilled things, and was a general nuisance. In fact, only Willibald's patience saved him from being sent home in disgrace.

Of course, Fritzl was very pleased to have most of the unpleasant chores done for him. He didn't have to dust, or sweep, or scrub, or fetch water for the tank in the sorcerer's cellar workshop. Willibald used a good deal of water in his spells. And all this happened in the days before there were such things as faucets and sinks and city water supplies.

But in spite of all this, Fritzl wasn't satisfied. There were times when the sorcerer would go away and leave him to do all the work himself. Fritzl disliked those days terribly. So he decided to learn the spell his master used on the furniture. One day he crept to the top of the cellar stairs and peeped over. Willibald was busy stirring something in a kettle over the fire.

He stopped stirring to reach for a piece of firewood, and then exclaimed, "Out of wood again! That boy! Fritzl! *Fritzl!*"

Fritzl trembled, but didn't answer. He was afraid his master would guess that he had been spying.

"Fritzl! Where *is* that boy? Never here when you want him." The sorcerer grumbled a bit. Then he stopped stir-

ring, and went over and stood a broom against the wall. He stepped back three paces, and forward two paces, and clapped his hands three times. Then he said, "Lif! Luf! Laf! Broom, fetch firewood!"

The broom immediately appeared to have arms—somewhat thin ones, and rather splintery, but still, arms. It came toward the stairs, hopping and thumping along on its straws. Willibald went back to his stirring, and Fritzl waited till the broom had thumped past his hiding place. Then he quietly crept away. Now he knew the spell, and he felt quite pleased with himself. He wouldn't have to work nearly so hard when old Willibald went off and left him to do everything alone.

There came a day when the sorcerer had to go off on business to the other side of town in a great hurry. In fact, he was almost tempted to travel in a puff of smoke instead

of on his donkey. But he remembered in time who he was and soon he and his donkey were clip-clopping down the street. But before he went, he said to Fritzl:

"This place is a mess. While I'm gone you set about clearing it out. And be sure to scrub the cellar floor clean. I dropped a spell I was mixing last night, and it's left quite a large stain. I'm expecting a visitor from the Sorcerer's Society of Silesia in a few days and I don't want him to think I'm in the habit of spilling things. And then don't forget to refill the water tub in the workshop." You see, Willibald was very vain of the reputation he had of being no ordinary sorcerer.

When his master had gone, Fritzl went to work with a broom. He swept clouds of dust—both star and earth—in all directions. Then he started on the furniture, wiping and polishing till everything shone. After that he went down-

stairs to the workshop and scrubbed the floor there. The stain was very large and very dark, and he scrubbed a long time. By the time he had finished, the water tub was empty. It was a warm day and he had worked very hard. The idea of making many trips to the river with the water bucket didn't appeal to him at all.

Then he had an idea: Why not let the broom fetch the water? Of course, if old Willibald found out, he would very likely be terribly angry. But surely the tub would be full by the time the sorcerer returned and no one would ever know. So Fritzl thought, and he wasted no time in thinking any further.

He seized the broom, stood it up against the wall, stepped back three paces, forward two paces, as he had seen Willibald do, then clapped his hands three times and said the magic words: "Lif! Luf! Laf! Broom, fetch water from the river!" He was delighted when the broom's arms appeared and it picked up the water bucket and started—thump-athump-athump!—up the stairs.

Soon it was back, and before Fritzl knew what was happening, it had tilted the bucket and flung the water across the room with a splash. Then it was off again—thump-athump-athump!—before Fritzl could stop it.

The water ran about and got in Fritzl's shoes, which wasn't very comfortable. He thought: "Well, perhaps I didn't

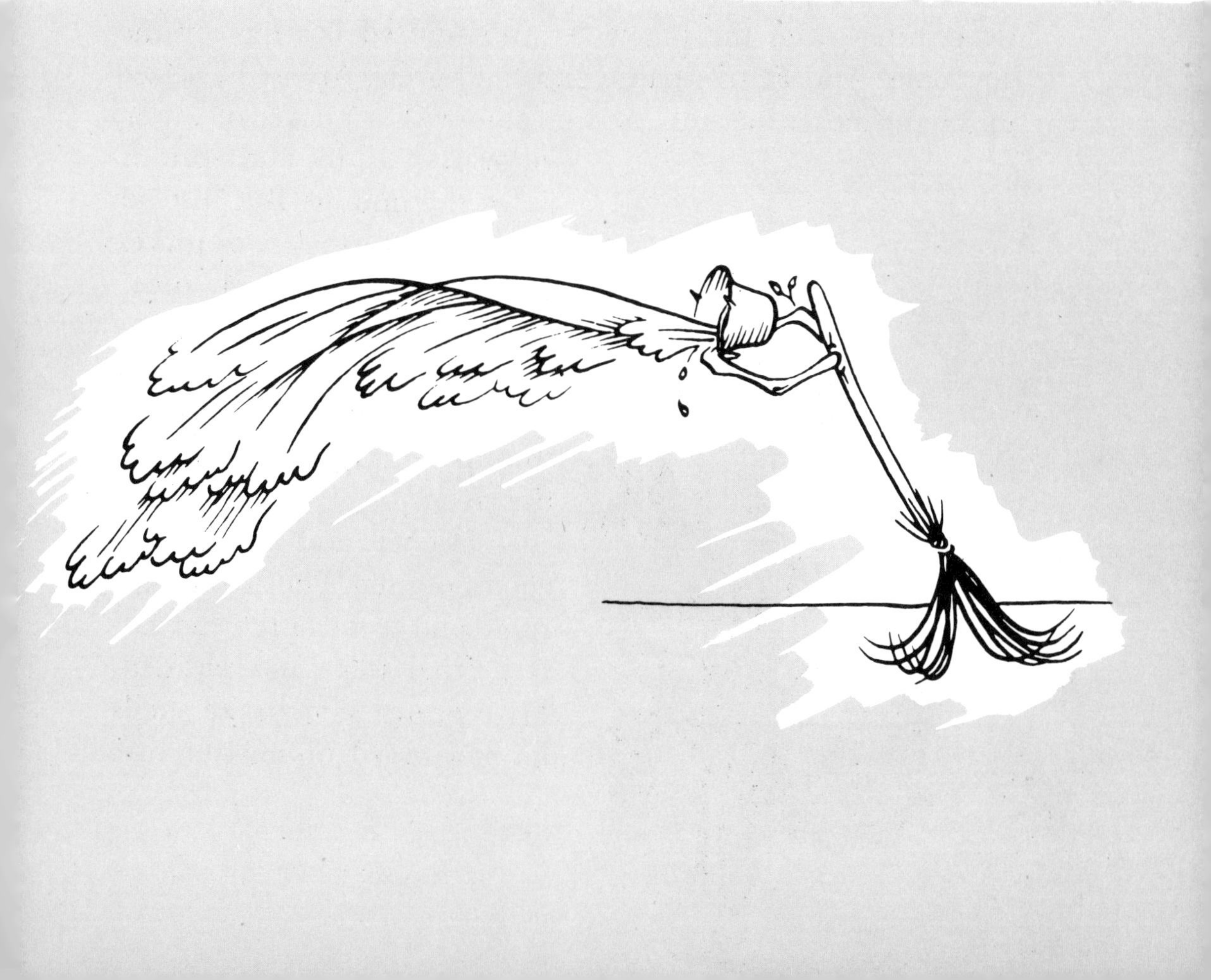

think fast enough. When it comes back I'll make it put the water in the tub instead of spilling it out on the floor."

Almost before he knew it, the broom had returned. As soon as it appeared at the top of the stairs with another bucket of water, Fritzl called out: "Don't throw it. Pour it in the tub!" But the broom paid no heed, flung the water as before, and went off—thump-athump-athump!—for more.

Poor Fritzl was frantic. "Something is wrong here," he thought. "Perhaps I'd better do the job myself and not try to get it done by magic." And when the broom returned again, he clapped his hands three times and cried: "Lif! Luf! Laf! Broom, stop fetching water!" But once more the broom paid no heed and flung the water across the room. And again it went off—thump-athump-athump!—for more.

Again and again the broom went back and forth, each time fetching and sloshing out a bucket of water and returning to the river for another. Fritzl became desperate. The water rose higher and higher until it reached his knees. Everything—even the big water tub—started floating around the room. And Fritzl's panic grew and grew. At last he seized an ax and next time the broom came with a bucket of water, he swung wildly and split it down the middle. But instead of stopping, the two pieces went merrily on. Each piece grew another arm, and another bucket appeared from nowhere. Off they went — thump-athump-athump! — to the river.

Higher and higher the flood mounted. The two brooms came and went faster and faster. Fritzl wept and pleaded. He repeated snatches of spells he had heard his master use.

He tried to get out of the cellar, but the water had floated the wooden steps out of place. The brooms went on and on and the water rose and rose.

Just as it rose to his chin, Fritzl heard the clip-clop of his master's donkey coming along the street. Then he heard the donkey stop and Willibald coming in the front door. "Help! Help!" he cried.

Willibald quickly appeared at the top of the stairs. "What goes on here?" he howled. Just then the brooms came in with more water and sloshed it down the stairs. Willibald was in the way and his gown was drenched. And there is nothing quite so angry as a wet sorcerer.

"Help, Master, quick!" poor Fritzl wailed. "I tried to make the broom fetch water, and then it wouldn't stop. Do something, before I drown!"

"Dumbhead!" roared Willibald. "I ought to let you drown. It's just what you deserve!" As he said this, he jumped hastily aside, for the brooms could be heard thump-athump-athump!-ing into the house. When they appeared, the sorcerer clapped his hands *four times*. Then he gabbled a long string of words. But Fritzl didn't hear them, for just then the water tub bumped against his head. He lost his footing and went under the water with a gurgle.

Next thing he knew, he was lying on the floor coughing and gasping. He looked around him. The water was gone. In fact, there wasn't anything in the cellar that was even wet. The steps were back in their places in the stairs. One broom stood quietly and peacefully in the woodbox, with a bucket beside it. The other broom and bucket had disappeared.

Fritzl looked fearfully up at his master. The sorcerer stood at the top of the stairs, sputtering and fuming with rage. "Get out of my sight, you blockhead! I've reached the end of my patience! Go on, get out! Go back where you came from!" And he clapped his hands quite a bit and stamped his foot—the left one—and a puff of smoke appeared on the floor beside Fritzl.

The puff of smoke grew and grew. As it grew it moved over and covered the apprentice. He shut his eyes in fright. He felt himself being lifted and heard a whistling in his ears like the wind. Then he was dropped with a hard bump. When he opened his eyes, he saw he was in his mother's front yard.

Fritzl lived to be a very old man, but he never saw the sorcerer again. And he didn't want to. In the fine summer evenings he would sit and tell stories to his grandchildren. They liked best the story of old Willibald and the broom. They remembered it and told it to their grandchildren. And *they* told it to *their* grandchildren. And so it has come down to us.

THE PIED PIPER OF HAMELIN

Hamelin Town's in Brunswick,
By famous Hanover city;
The river Weser, deep and wide,
Washes its wall on the southern side;
A pleasanter spot you never spied;
But, when begins my ditty,
Almost five hundred years ago,
To see the townsfolk suffer so
From vermin, was a pity.

Rats!
They fought the dogs and killed the cats,
And bit the babies in the cradles,
And ate the cheeses out of the vats.
And licked the soup from the cook's own ladles,
Split open the kegs of salted sprats,
Made nests inside men's Sunday hats,
And even spoiled the women's chats,
By drowning their speaking
With shrieking and squeaking
In fifty different sharps and flats.
At last the people in a body
To the Town Hall came flocking:
" 'Tis clear," cried they, "our Mayor's a noddy;
"And as for our Corporation–shocking
"To think we buy gowns lined with ermine

"For dolts that can't or won't determine
"What's best to rid us of our vermin!
"You hope, because you're old and obese,
"To find in the furry civic robe ease?
"Rouse up, sirs! Give your brains a racking
"To find the remedy we're lacking,
"Or, sure as fate, we'll send you packing!"
At this the Mayor and Corporation
Quaked with a mighty consternation.

An hour they sat in council,
  At length the Mayor broke silence:
"For a guilder I'd my ermine gown sell;
  "I wish I were a mile hence!
"It's easy to bid one rack one's brain—
"Im sure my poor head aches again,
"I've scratched it so, and all in vain.
"Oh for a trap, a trap, a trap!"
Just as he said this, what should hap
At the chamber door but a gentle tap?
"Bless us," cried the Mayor, "what's that?"
(With the Corporation as he sat,
Looking little though wondrous fat;
Nor brighter was his eye, nor moister
Than a too-long-opened oyster,
Save when at noon his paunch grew mutinous
For a plate of turtle green and glutinous)
"Only a scraping of shoes on the mat?

"Anything like the sound of a rat
"Makes my heart go pit-a-pat!"

"Come in!"—the Mayor cried, looking bigger:
And in did come the strangest figure!
His queer long coat from heel to head
Was half of yellow and half of red,
And he himself was tall and thin,
With sharp blue eyes, each like a pin,
And light loose hair, yet swarthy skin
No tuft on cheek nor beard on chin,
But lips where smiles went out and in;
There was no guessing his kith and kin:
And nobody could enough admire
The tall man and his quaint attire.
Quoth one: "It's as my great-grandsire,
"Starting up at the Trump of Doom's tone,
"Had walked this way from his painted tombstone!"

He advanced to the council-table:
And, "Please your honours," said he, "I'm able,

"By means of a secret charm, to draw
"All creatures living beneath the sun,
"That creep or swim or fly or run,
"After me so as you never saw!
"And I chiefly use my charm
"On creatures that do people harm,
"The mole and toad and newt and viper;
"And people call me the Pied Piper."
(And here they noticed round his neck
A scarf of red and yellow stripe,
To match with his coat of the self-same cheque;
And at the scarf's end hung a pipe;
And his fingers they noticed were ever straying
As if impatient to be playing
Upon this pipe, as low it dangled
Over his vesture so old-fangled.)
"Yet," said he, "poor Piper as I am,
"In Tartary I freed the Cham,
"Last June, from his huge swarms of gnats,
"I eased in Asia the Nizam
"Of a monstrous brood of vampyre-bats:
"And as for what your brain bewilders,
"If I can rid your town of rats
"Will you give me a thousand guilders?"

"One? fifty thousand!"—was the exclamation
Of the astonished Mayor and Corporation.

Into the street the Piper stept,
  Smiling first a little smile,
As if he knew what magic slept
  In his quiet pipe the while;
Then, like a musical adept,
To blow the pipe his lips he wrinkled,
And green and blue his sharp eyes twinkled,
Like a candle-flame where salt is sprinkled;
And ere three shrill notes the pipe uttered,
You heard as if an army muttered;
And the muttering grew to a grumbling;
And the grumbling grew to a mighty rumbling;
And out of the houses the rats came tumbling.
Great rats, small rats, lean rats, brawny rats,
Brown rats, black rats, grey rats, tawny rats,
Grave old plodders, gay young friskers,
  Fathers, mothers, uncles, cousins,
Cocking tails and pricking whiskers,
  Families by tens and dozens,

Brothers, sisters, husbands, wives—
Followed the Piper for their lives.
From street to street he piped advancing,
And step for step they followed dancing,
Until they came to the river Weser
Wherein all plunged and perished!
—Save one who, stout as Julius Caesar,
Swam across and lived to carry
(As he, the manuscript he cherished)
To Rat-land home his commentary:
Which was, "At the first shrill notes of the pipe,
"I heard a sound as of scraping tripe,
"And putting apples, wondrous ripe,
"Into a cider-press's gripe:
"And a moving away of pickle-tub-boards,
"And a leaving ajar of conserve-cupboards,
"And a drawing the corks of train-oil-flasks,
"And a breaking the hoops of butter-casks:
"And it seemed as if a voice
" (Sweeter far than by harp or by psaltery
"Is breathed) called out, 'Oh rats, rejoice!
" 'The world is grown to one vast drysaltery!
" 'So munch on, crunch on, take your nuncheon,

" 'Breakfast, supper, dinner, luncheon!'
"And just as a bulky sugar-puncheon,
"All ready staved, like a great sun shone
"Glorious scarce an inch before me,
"Just as methought it said, 'Come, bore me!'
"—I found the Weser rolling o'er me."

You should have heard the Hamelin people
Ringing the bells till they rocked the steeple.
"Go," cried the Mayor, "and get long poles,
"Poke out the nests and block up the holes!
"Consult with carpenters and builders,
"And leave in our town not even a trace
"Of the rats!"—when suddenly, up the face
Of the Piper perked in the market-place,
With a, "First, if you please, my thousand guilders!"

A thousand guilders! The Mayor looked blue;
So did the Corporation too.
For council dinners made rare havoc
With Claret, Moselle, Vin-de-Grave, Hock;
And half the money would replenish
Their cellar's biggest butt with Rhenish.
To pay this sum to a wandering fellow
With a gipsy coat of red and yellow!
"Beside," quoth the Mayor with a knowing wink,
"Our business was done at the river's brink;
"We saw with our eyes the vermin sink,
"And what's dead can't come to life, I think.
"So, friend, we're not the folks to shrink
"From the duty of giving you something to drink,
"And a matter of money to put in your poke;
"But as for the guilders, what we spoke
"Of them, as you very well know, was in joke.

"Beside, our losses have made us thrifty.
"A thousand guilders! Come, take fifty!"

The Piper's face fell, and he cried,
"No trifling! I can't wait, beside!
"I've promised to visit by dinner-time
"Bagdad, and accept the prime
"Of the Head-Cook's pottage, all he's rich in,
"For having left, in the Caliph's kitchen,
"Of a nest of scorpions no survivor:
"With him I proved no bargain-driver,
"With you, don't think I'll bate a stiver!
"And folks who put me in a passion
"May find me pipe after another fashion."

"How?" cried the Mayor, "d' ye think I brook
"Being worse treated than a Cook?
"Insulted by a lazy ribald
"With idle pipe and vesture piebald?
"You threaten us, fellow? Do your worst,
"Blow your pipe there till you burst!"

Once more he stept into the street,
  And to his lips again
Laid his long pipe of smooth straight cane;
And ere he blew three notes (such sweet
Soft notes as yet musician's cunning
  Never gave the enraptured air)

There was a rustling,
That seemed like a bustling
Of merry crowds justling at pitching and hustling,
Small feet were pattering, wooden shoes clattering,
Little hands clapping and little tongues chattering,
And, like fowls in a farm-yard when barley is scattering,
Out came the children running.
All the little boys and girls,
With rosy cheeks and flaxen curls,
And sparkling eyes and teeth like pearls,
Tripping
and skipping,
ran merrily after
The wonderful music with
shouting and laughter.

The Mayor was dumb, and the Council stood
As if they were changed into blocks of wood,
Unable to move a step, or cry
To the children merrily skipping by
—Could only follow with the eye
That joyous crowd at the Piper's back.
But how the Mayor was on the rack,
And the wretched Council's bosoms beat,
As the Piper turned from the High Street
To where the Weser rolled its waters
Right in the way of their sons and daughters!
However he turned from South to West,
And to Koppelberg Hill his steps addressed,
And after him the children pressed;
Great was the joy in every breast.
"He never can cross that mighty top!
"He's forced to let the piping drop,
"And we shall see our children stop!"
When, lo, as they reached the mountain-side,
A wondrous portal opened wide,

As if a cavern was suddenly hollowed;
And the Piper advanced and the children followed.
And when all were in to the very last,
The door in the mountain-side shut fast.
Did I say, all? No! One was lame,
And could not dance the whole of the way;
And in after years, if you would blame
His sadness, he was used to say,—
"It's dull in our town since my playmates left!
"I can't forget that I'm bereft
"Of all the pleasant sights they see,
"Which the Piper also promised me.
"For he led us, he said, to a joyous land,
"Joining the town and just at hand,
"Where waters gushed and fruit-trees grew,
"And flowers put forth a fairer hue,
"And everything was strange and new;
"The sparrows were brighter than peacocks here,
"And their dogs outran our fallow deer,
"And honey-bees had lost their stings,
"And horses were born with eagles' wings;
"And just as I became assured
"My lame foot would be speedily cured,
"The music stopped and I stood still,
"And found myself outside the hill,
"Left alone against my will,

"To go now limping as before,
"And never hear of that country more!"

Alas, alas for Hamelin!
  There came into many a burgher's pate
  A text which says that Heaven's gate
  Opes to the rich at as easy rate
As the needle's eye takes a camel in!
The Mayor sent East, West, North, and South,
To offer the Piper, by word of mouth,
  Wherever it was men's lot to find him,
Silver and gold to his heart's content,
If he'd only return the way he went,
  And bring the children behind him.
But when they saw 'twas a lost endeavour,
And Piper and dancers were gone for ever,
They made a decree that lawyers never
  Should think their records dated duly
If, after the day of the month and year,
These words did not as well appear,
"And so long after what happened here
  "On the Twenty-second of July,
"Thirteen hundred and seventy-six:"
And the better in memory to fix

The place of the children's last retreat,
They called it, the Pied Piper's Street—
Where any one playing on pipe or tabor,
Was sure for the future to lose his labour.
Nor suffered they hostelry or tavern
  To shock with mirth a street so solemn;
But opposite the place of the cavern
  They wrote the story on a column,
And on the great church-window painted
The same, to make the world acquainted
How their children were stolen away,
And there it stands to this very day.
And I must not omit to say
That in Transylvania there's a tribe
Of alien people that ascribe
The outlandish ways and dress
On which their neighbours lay such stress,
To their fathers and mothers having risen
Out of some subterraneous prison
Into which they were trepanned
Long time ago in a mighty band
Out of Hamelin town in Brunswick land,
But how or why, they don't understand.

Robert Browning

Rip Van Winkle

By Washington Irving

WHOEVER HAS MADE a voyage up the Hudson must remember the Kaatskill Mountains. They are a dismembered branch of the great Appalachian family, and are seen away

to the west of the river, swelling up to a noble height and lording it over the surrounding country. Every change of season, every change of weather, indeed, every hour of the day produces some change in the magical hues and shapes of these mountains, and they are regarded by all the good wives, far and near, as perfect barometers. When the weather is fair and settled, they are clothed in blue and purple, and print their bold outlines on the clear evening sky; but, sometimes, when the rest of the landscape is cloudless, they will gather a hood of gray vapors about their summits, which, in the last rays of the setting sun, will glow and light up like a crown of glory.

At the foot of these fairy mountains, the voyager may have descried the light smoke curling up from a village, whose shingle roofs gleam among the trees, just where the blue tints of the upland melt away into the fresh green of the nearer landscape. It is a little village of great antiquity, having been founded by some of the Dutch colonists in the early times of the province, just about the beginning of the government of the good Peter Stuyvesant (may he rest in peace!), and there were some of the houses of the original settlers standing within a few years, built of small yellow bricks brought from Holland, having latticed windows and gable fronts, surmounted with weathercocks.

In that same village, and in one of these very houses (which, to tell the precise truth, was sadly time-worn and weather-beaten), there lived many years since, while the country was yet a province of Great Britain, a simple, good-natured fellow of the name of Rip Van Winkle. He was a descendant of the Van Winkles who figured so gallantly in the chivalrous days of Peter Stuyvesant, and accompanied him to the siege of Fort Christina. He inherited, however, but little of the martial character of his ancestors. I have observed that he was a simple, good-natured man; he was, moreover, a kind neighbor, and an obedient, henpecked husband. Indeed, to the latter circumstance might be owing that meekness of spirit which gained him such universal popularity, for those men are most apt to be obsequious and conciliating abroad who are under the discipline of shrews at home. Their tempers, doubtless, are rendered pliant and malleable in the fiery furnace of domestic tribulation, and a curtain lecture is worth all the sermons in the world for teaching the virtues of patience and long-suffer-ing. A termagant wife may, therefore, in some respects, be considered a tolerable blessing; and if so, Rip Van Winkle was thrice blessed.

Certain it is that he was a great favorite among all the good wives of the village, who, as usual with the amiable sex, took his part in all family squabbles and never failed, whenever they talked those matters over in their evening gossipings, to lay all the blame on Dame Van Winkle. The children of the village, too, would shout with joy whenever he approached. He assisted at their sports, made their playthings, taught them to fly kites and shoot marbles, and told them long stories of ghosts, witches, and Indians. Whenever he went dodging about the village, he was surrounded by a troop of them, hanging on his skirts, clambering on his back, and playing a thousand tricks on him with impunity; and not a dog would bark at him throughout the neighborhood.

The great error in Rip's composition was an insuperable aversion to all kinds of profitable labor. It could not be from the want of assiduity or perseverance, for he would sit on a wet rock, with a rod as long and heavy as a Tartar's lance, and fish all day without a murmur, even though he should not be encouraged by a single nibble. He would carry a fowling piece on his shoulder for hours together, trudging through woods

and swamps and up hill and down dale to shoot a few squirrels or wild pigeons. He would never refuse to assist a neighbor even in the roughest toil, and was a foremost man at all country frolics for husking Indian corn or building stone fences; the women of the village, too, used to employ him to run their errands and to do such little odd jobs as their less obliging husbands would not do for them. In a word, Rip was ready to attend to anybody's business but his own; but as to doing family duty and keeping his farm in order, he found it impossible.

In fact, he declared it was of no use to work on his farm; it was the most pestilent little piece of ground in the whole country; everything about it went wrong, and would go wrong, in spite of him. His fences were continually falling to pieces; his cow would either go astray or get among the cabbages; weeds were sure to grow quicker in his fields than anywhere else; the rain always made a point of setting in just as he had

some outdoor work to do; so that though his patrimonial estate had dwindled away under his management, acre by acre, until there was little more left than a mere patch of Indian corn and potatoes, yet it was the worst-conditioned farm in the neighborhood.

His children, too, were as ragged and wild as if they belonged to nobody. His son Rip, an urchin begotten in his own likeness, promised to inherit the habits, with the old clothes, of his father. He was generally seen trooping like a colt at his mother's heels, equipped in a pair of his father's cast-off galligaskins, which he had much ado to hold up with one hand as a fine lady does her train in bad weather.

Rip Van Winkle, however, was one of those happy mortals of foolish, well-oiled dispositions who take the world easy, eat white bread or brown, whichever can be got with least thought or trouble, and would rather starve on a penny than work for a pound. If left to himself, he would have whistled life away in perfect contentment; but his wife kept continually dinning in his ears about his idleness, his carelessness, and the ruin he was bringing on his family. Morning, noon, and night, her tongue was incessantly going, and everything he said or did was sure to produce a torrent of household eloquence. Rip had but one way of replying to all lectures of the kind, and

that, by frequent use, had grown into a habit. He shrugged his shoulders, shook his head, cast up his eyes, but said nothing. This, however, always provoked a fresh volley from his wife, so that he was fain to draw off his forces and take to the outside of the house—the only side which, in truth, belongs to a henpecked husband.

Rip's sole domestic adherent was his dog, Wolf, who was as much henpecked as his master, for Dame Van Winkle regarded them as companions in idleness, and even looked upon

Wolf with an evil eye as the cause of his master's going so often astray. True it is, in all points of spirit befitting an honorable dog, he was as courageous an animal as ever scoured the woods —but what courage can withstand the ever-during and all-besetting terrors of a woman's tongue? The moment Wolf entered the house his crest fell, his tail drooped to the ground, or curled between his legs, he sneaked about with a gallows air, casting many a sidelong glance at Dame Van Winkle, and at the least flourish of a broomstick or ladle he would fly to the door with yelping precipitation.

Times grew worse and worse with Rip Van Winkle as years of matrimony rolled on; a tart temper never mellows with age, and a sharp tongue is the only edged tool that grows keener with constant use. For a long while he used to console himself, when driven from home, by frequenting a kind of perpetual club of the sages, philosophers, and other idle personages of the village, which held its sessions on a bench before a small inn, designated by a rubicund portrait of His Majesty George the Third. Here they used to sit in the shade through a long, lazy summer's day, talking listlessly over village gossip or telling endless sleepy stories about nothing. But it would have been worth any statesman's money to have heard the profound discussions that sometimes took place when by chance an old newspaper fell into their hands from some passing traveler. How solemnly they would listen to the contents, as drawled out by Derrick Van Bummel, the schoolmaster, a dapper, learned little man who was not to be daunted by the most gigantic word in the dictionary; and how sagely they would deliberate upon public events some months after they had taken place.

The opinions of this junto were completely controlled by Nicholas Vedder, a patriarch of the village and landlord of the inn, at the door of which he took his seat from morning till night, just moving sufficiently to avoid the sun and keep in the shade of a large tree, so that the neighbors could tell the hour by his movements as accurately as by a sundial. It is true he was rarely heard to speak, but smoked his pipe incessantly. His adherents, however (for every great man has his adherents), perfectly understood him, and knew how to gather his opinions. When anything that was read or related displeased him, he was observed to smoke his pipe vehemently and to send forth short, frequent, and angry puffs; but when pleased, he would inhale the smoke slowly and tranquilly and emit it in light and placid clouds, and sometimes, taking the pipe from his mouth and letting the fragrant vapor curl about his nose, would gravely nod his head in token of perfect approbation.

From even this stronghold the unlucky Rip was at length routed by his termagant wife, who would suddenly break in upon the tranquillity of the assemblage and call the members all to naught; nor was that august personage, Nicholas Vedder himself, sacred from the daring tongue of this terrible virago, who charged him outright with encouraging her husband in habits of idleness.

Poor Rip was at last reduced almost to despair, and his only alternative, to escape from the labor of the farm and clamor of his wife, was to take gun in hand and stroll away into the woods. Here he would sometimes seat himself at the foot of a tree and share the contents of his wallet with Wolf, with whom he sympathized as a fellow sufferer in persecution. "Poor Wolf," he would say, "thy mistress leads thee a dog's life of it; but never mind, my lad, whilst I live thou shalt never want a friend to stand by thee!" Wolf would wag his tail, look wistfully in his master's face, and if dogs can feel pity, I verily believe he reciprocated the sentiment with all his heart.

In a long ramble of the kind of a fine autumnal day, Rip had unconsciously scrambled to one of the highest parts of the Kaatskill Mountains. He was after his favorite sport of squirrel shooting, and the still solitudes had echoed and re-echoed with the reports of his gun. Panting and fatigued, he threw himself, late in the afternoon, on a green knoll, covered with mountain herbage, that crowned the brow of a precipice. From an opening between the trees he could overlook all the lower country for many a mile of rich woodland. He saw at a distance the lordly Hudson, far, far below him, moving on its silent but majestic course, with the reflection of a purple cloud or the sail of a lagging bark here and there sleeping on its glassy bosom, and at last losing itself in the blue highlands.

On the other side he looked down into a deep mountain glen, wild, lonely, and shagged, the bottom filled with fragments from the impending cliffs, and scarcely lighted by the reflected rays of the setting sun. For some time Rip lay musing on this scene. Evening was gradually advancing; the mountains began to throw their long blue shadows over the valleys. He saw that it would be dark long before he could reach the village, and he heaved a heavy sigh when he thought of encountering the terrors of Dame Van Winkle.

As he was about to descend, he heard a voice from a distance, hallooing, "Rip Van Winkle! Rip Van Winkle!" He looked around, but could see nothing but a crow winging its solitary flight across the mountain. He thought his fancy must have deceived him, and turned again to descend, when he heard the same cry ring through the still evening air, "Rip Van Winkle! Rip Van Winkle!" At the same time Wolf bristled up his back and, giving a low growl, skulked to his master's side, looking fearfully down into the glen. Rip now felt a vague apprehension stealing over him; he looked anxiously in the same direction and perceived a strange figure slowly toiling up the rocks, and bending under the weight of something he carried on his back. He was surprised to see any human being in this lonely and unfrequented place, but supposing it to be some one of the neighborhood in need of his assistance, he hastened down to yield it.

On nearer approach he was still more surprised at the singularity of the stranger's appearance. He was a short, square-built old fellow, with thick, bushy hair and a grizzled beard. His dress was of the antique Dutch fashion—a cloth jerkin strapped around the waist and several pairs of breeches, the outer one of ample volume, decorated with rows of buttons down the sides and bunches at the knees. He bore on his shoulder a stout keg that seemed full of liquor, and made signs

for Rip to approach and assist him with the load. Though rather shy and distrustful of this new acquaintance, Rip complied with his usual alacrity, and mutually relieving one another, they clambered up a narrow gully, apparently the dry bed of a mountain torrent. As they ascended, Rip every now and then heard long rolling peals, like distant thunder, that seemed to issue out of a deep ravine, or rather cleft, between lofty rocks, toward which their rugged path conducted. He paused for an instant, but supposing it to be the muttering of one of those transient thunder showers which often take place in mountain heights, he proceeded. Passing through the ravine, they came to a hollow, like a small amphitheater, surrounded by perpendicular precipices, over the brinks of which impending trees shot their branches, so that you only caught glimpses of the azure sky and the bright evening cloud. During the whole time, Rip and his companion had labored on in silence, for though the former marveled greatly what could be the object of carrying a keg of liquor up this wild mountain, yet there was something strange and incomprehensible about the unknown that inspired awe and checked familiarity.

On entering the amphitheater, new objects of wonder were to be seen. On a level spot in the center was a company of odd-looking personages playing at ninepins. They were dressed in a quaint, outlandish fashion; some wore short doublets, others jerkins, with long knives in their belts, and most of them had enormous breeches, of similar style with that of the guide's. Their visages, too, were peculiar; one had a large beard, broad face, and small piggish eyes, the face of another seemed to consist entirely of nose and was surmounted by a white sugar-loaf hat set off with a little red cock's tail. They all had beards, of various shapes and colors. There was one who seemed to be the commander. He was a stout old gentleman, with a weather-beaten countenance; he wore a laced doublet, broad belt and hanger, high-crowned hat and feather, red stockings, and high-heeled shoes, with roses in them. The whole group reminded Rip of the figures in an old

Flemish painting, in the parlor of Dominie Van Shaick, the village parson, and which had been brought over from Holland at the time of the settlement.

What seemed particularly odd to Rip was that though these folks were evidently amusing themselves, yet they maintained the gravest faces, the most mysterious silence, and were, withal, the most melancholy party of pleasure he had ever witnessed. Nothing interrupted the stillness of the scene but the noise of the balls, which, whenever they were rolled, echoed along the mountains like rumbling peals of thunder.

As Rip and his companion approached them, they suddenly desisted from their play and stared at him with such fixed, statuelike gaze and such strange, uncouth, lackluster countenances that his heart turned within him and his knees smote together. His companion now emptied the contents of the keg into large flagons and made signs to him to wait upon the company. He obeyed with fear and trembling; they quaffed the liquor in profound silence and then returned to their game.

By degrees Rip's awe and apprehension subsided. He even ventured, when no eye was fixed upon him, to taste the

beverage, which he found had much of the flavor of excellent Hollands. He was naturally a thirsty soul and was soon tempted to repeat the draft. One taste provoked another; and he reiterated his visits to the flagon so often that at length his senses were overpowered, his eyes swam in his head, his head gradually declined, and he fell into a deep sleep.

On waking, he found himself on the green knoll whence he had first seen the old man of the glen. He rubbed his eyes—it was a bright, sunny morning. The birds were hopping and twittering among the bushes, and the eagle was wheeling aloft and breasting the pure mountain breeze. "Surely," thought Rip, "I have not slept here all night." He recalled the occurrences before he fell asleep. The strange man with a keg of liquor—the mountain ravine—the wild retreat among the rocks—the woebegone party at ninepins—the flagon—"Oh! That flagon! That wicked flagon!" thought Rip. "What excuse shall I make to Dame Van Winkle?"

He looked around for his gun, but in place of the clean, well-oiled fowling piece he found an old firelock lying by him, the barrel encrusted with rust, the lock falling off, and the stock worm-eaten. He now suspected that the grave roysters of the mountain had put a trick upon him, and, having dosed him with liquor, had robbed him of his gun. Wolf, too, had disappeared, but he might have strayed away after a squirrel or partridge. He whistled after him and shouted his name, but all in vain; the echoes repeated his whistle and shout, but no dog was to be seen.

He determined to revisit the scene of the last evening's gambol, and if he met with any of the party, to demand his dog and gun. As he rose to walk, he found himself stiff in the joints and wanting in his usual activity. "These mountain beds do not agree with me," thought Rip, "and if this frolic should lay me up with a fit of the rheumatism, I shall have a blessed time with Dame Van Winkle." With some difficulty he got down into the glen; he found the gully up which he and his companion had ascended the preceding evening, but to his astonishment a mountain stream was now foaming down it, leaping from rock to rock and filling the glen with babbling murmurs. He, however, made shift to scramble up its sides, working his toilsome way through thickets of birch, sassafras, and witch hazel, and sometimes tripped up or entangled by the wild grapevines that twisted their coils or tendrils from tree to tree and spread a kind of network in his path.

At length he reached to where the ravine had opened through the cliffs to the amphitheater, but no traces of such opening remained. The rocks presented a high, impenetrable wall over which the torrent came tumbling in a sheet of feathery foam and fell into a broad, deep basin, black from the shadows of the surrounding forest. Here, then, poor Rip was brought to a stand. He again called and whistled after his dog; he was only answered by the cawing of a flock of idle crows, sporting high in air about a dry tree that overhung a sunny precipice, and who, secure in their elevation, seemed to look down and scoff at the poor man's perplexities. What was to be done? The morning was passing away, and Rip felt famished for want of his breakfast. He grieved to give up his dog and gun; he dreaded to meet his wife, but it would not do to starve among the mountains. He shook his head, shouldered the rusty firelock, and, with a heart full of trouble and anxiety, turned his steps homeward.

As he approached the village he met a number of people, but none whom he knew, which somewhat surprised him, for he had thought himself acquainted with every one in the country around. Their dress, too, was of a different fashion from that to which he was accustomed. They all stared at him with equal marks of surprise, and whenever they cast their eyes upon him invariably stroked their chins. The constant recurrence of this gesture induced Rip, involuntarily, to do the same, when, to his astonishment, he found his beard had grown a foot long!

He had now entered the skirts of the village. A troop of strange children ran at his heels, hooting after him and pointing at his gray beard. The dogs, too, not one of which he recognized for an old acquaintance, barked at him as he passed. The very village was altered; it was larger and more populous. There were rows of houses which he had never seen before, and those which had been his familiar haunts had disappeared.

Strange names were over the doors—strange faces at the windows—everything was strange. His mind now misgave him; he began to doubt whether both he and the world around him were not bewitched. Surely this was his native village, which he had left but the day before. There stood the Kaatskill Mountains—there ran the silver Hudson at a distance—there was every hill and dale precisely as it had always been. Rip was sorely perplexed. "That flagon last night," thought he, "has addled my poor head sadly!"

It was with some difficulty that he found the way to his own house, which he approached with silent awe, expecting every moment to hear the shrill voice of Dame Van Winkle. He found the house gone to decay—the roof fallen in, the windows shattered, and the doors off the hinges. A half-starved dog that looked like Wolf was skulking about it. Rip called him by name, but the cur snarled, showed his teeth, and passed

on. This was an unkind cut indeed. "My very dog," sighed poor Rip, "has forgotten me!"

He entered the house, which, to tell the truth, Dame Van Winkle had always kept in neat order. It was empty, forlorn, and apparently abandoned. This desolateness overcame all his connubial fears—he called loudly for his wife and children; the lonely chambers rang for a moment with his voice, and then all again was silence.

He now hurried forth and hastened to his old resort, the village inn—but it too was gone. A large, rickety, wooden building stood in its place, with great gaping windows, some of them broken and mended with old hats and petticoats, and over the door was painted, "the Union Hotel, by Jonathan Doolittle." Instead of the great tree that used to shelter the quiet little Dutch inn of yore, there now was reared a tall, naked pole, with something on the top that looked like a red nightcap, and from it was fluttering a flag, on which was a singular assemblage of stars and stripes—all this was strange and incomprehensible. He recognized on the sign, however, the ruby face of King George, under which he had smoked so many a peaceful pipe; but even this was singularly metamorphosed. The red coat was changed for one of blue and buff, a sword was held in the hand instead of a scepter, the head was decorated with a cocked hat, and underneath was painted in large characters, GENERAL WASHINGTON.

There was, as usual, a crowd of folk about the door, but none that Rip recollected. The very character of the people seemed changed. There was a busy, bustling, disputatious tone about it, instead of the accustomed phlegm and drowsy tranquillity. He looked in vain for the sage Nicholas Vedder, with his broad face, double chin, and fair long pipe, uttering clouds of tobacco smoke instead of idle speeches; or Van Bummel, the schoolmaster, doling forth the contents of an ancient newspaper. In place of these, a lean, bilious-looking fellow, with his pockets full of handbills, was haranguing vehemently about rights of citizens—elections—members of congress—liberty—Bunker's Hill—heroes of seventy-six—and other words, which were a perfect Babylonish jargon to the bewildered Van Winkle.

The appearance of Rip, with his long, grizzled beard, his rusty fowling piece, his uncouth dress, and an army of women and children at his heels, soon attracted the attention of the tavern politicians. They crowded around him, eying him from head to foot with great curiosity. The orator bustled up to him and, drawing him partly aside, inquired "on which side he voted?" Rip stared in vacant stupidity. Another short but busy little fellow pulled him by the arm, and, rising on tiptoe, inquired in his ear, "whether he was Federal or Democrat?" Rip was equally at a loss to comprehend the question; when a knowing, self-important old gentleman in a sharp cocked hat made his way through the crowd, putting them to the right and left with his elbows as he passed, and, planting himself before Van Winkle, with one arm akimbo, the other resting on his cane, his keen eyes and sharp hat penetrating, as it were, into his very soul, demanded in an austere tone, "what brought him to the election with a gun on his shoulder, and a mob at his heels, and whether he meant to breed a riot in the village?" "Alas! Gentlemen," cried Rip, somewhat dismayed, "I am a poor, quiet man, a native of the place, and a loyal subject of the king, God bless him!"

Here a general shout burst from the bystanders. "A tory!

A tory! A spy! A refugee! Hustle him! Away with him!" It was with great difficulty that the self-important man in the cocked hat restored order; and, having assumed a tenfold austerity of brow, demanded again of the unknown culprit what he came there for and whom he was seeking. The poor man humbly assured him that he meant no harm, but merely came there in search of some of his neighbors, who used to keep about the tavern.

"Well—who are they? Name them."

Rip bethought himself a moment, and inquired, "Where's Nicholas Vedder?"

There was a silence for a little while, when an old man replied, in a thin, piping voice, "Nicholas Vedder! Why, he is dead and gone these eighteen years! There was a wooden tombstone in the churchyard that used to tell all about him, but that's rotten and gone too."

"Where's Brom Dutcher?"

"Oh, he went off to the army in the beginning of the war; some say he was killed at the storming of Stony Point—others say he was drowned in a squall at the foot of Antony's Nose. I don't know—he never came back again."

"Where's Van Bummel, the schoolmaster?"

"He went off to the wars, too, was a great militia general, and is now in congress."

Rip's heart died away at hearing of these sad changes in his home and friends, and finding himself thus alone in the world. Every answer puzzled him, too, by treating of such enormous lapses of time and of matters which he could not understand: war—congress—Stony Point. He had no courage to ask after any more friends, but cried out in despair, "Does nobody here know Rip Van Winkle?"

"Oh, Rip Van Winkle!" exclaimed two or three. "Oh, to be sure! That's Rip Van Winkle yonder, leaning against the tree."

Rip looked, and beheld a precise counterpart of himself as he went up the mountain: apparently as lazy, and certainly as ragged. The poor fellow was now completely confounded. He doubted his own identity, whether he was himself or another man. In the midst of his bewilderment, the man in the cocked hat demanded who he was, and what was his name?

"God knows," exclaimed he, at his wit's end. "I'm not myself—I'm somebody else—that's me yonder—no—that's somebody else got into my shoes—I was myself last night, but I fell asleep on the mountain, and they've changed my gun, and everything's changed, and I'm changed, and I can't tell what's my name, or who I am!"

The bystanders began now to look at each other, nod, wink significantly, and tap their fingers against their foreheads. There was a whisper also about securing the gun and keeping the old fellow from doing mischief, at the very suggestion of which the self-important man in the cocked hat retired with some precipitation. At this critical moment a fresh, comely woman pressed through the throng to get a peep at the gray-bearded man. She had a chubby child in her arms, which, frightened at his looks, began to cry. "Hush, Rip," cried she, "hush, you little fool; the old man won't hurt you." The name of the child, the air of the mother, the tone of her voice, all awakened a train of recollections in his mind. "What is your name, my good woman?" asked he.

"Judith Gardenier."

"And your father's name?"

"Ah, poor man, Rip Van Winkle was his name, but it's twenty years since he went away from home with his gun, and never has been heard of since—his dog came home without him; but whether he shot himself, or was carried away by the Indians, nobody can tell. I was then but a little girl."

Rip had but one question more to ask; but he put it with a faltering voice:

"Where's your mother?"

"Oh, she too had died but a short time since; she broke a blood vessel in a fit of passion at a New England peddler."

There was a drop of comfort, at least, in this intelligence. The honest man could contain himself no longer. He caught his daughter and her child in his arms. "I am your father!" cried he. "Young Rip Van Winkle once—old Rip Van Winkle now! Does nobody know poor Rip Van Winkle?"

All stood amazed, until an old woman, tottering out from among the crowd, put her hand to her brow and, peering under it in his face for a moment, exclaimed, "Sure enough! It is Rip Van Winkle—it is himself! Welcome home again, old neighbor. Why, where have you been these twenty long years?"

Rip's story was soon told, for the whole twenty years had been to him but as one night. The neighbors stared when they heard it; some were seen to wink at each other and put their tongues in their cheeks, and the self-important man in the cocked hat, who, when the alarm was over, had returned to the field, screwed down the corners of his mouth and shook his

head—upon which there was a general shaking of the head throughout the assemblage.

It was determined, however, to take the opinion of old Peter Vanderdonk, who was seen slowly advancing up the road. He was a descendant of the historian of that name, who wrote one of the earliest accounts of the province. Peter was the most ancient inhabitant of the village, and well versed in all the wonderful events and traditions of the neighborhood. He recollected Rip at once and corroborated his story in the most satisfactory manner. He assured the company that it was a fact, handed down from his ancestor the historian, that the Kaatskill Mountains had always been haunted by strange beings. That it was affirmed that the great Hendrick Hudson, the first discoverer of the river and country, kept a kind of vigil there every twenty years, with his crew of the *Half Moon,* being permitted in this way to revisit the scenes of his enterprise and keep a guardian eye upon the river and the great city called by his name. That his father had once seen them in their old Dutch dresses playing at ninepins in a hollow of the mountain, and that he himself had heard, one summer afternoon, the sound of their balls, like distant peals of thunder.

To make a long story short, the company broke up and returned to the more important concerns of the election. Rip's daughter took him home to live with her; she had a snug, well-furnished house, and a stout, cheery farmer for a husband, whom Rip recollected for one of the urchins that used to climb upon his back. As to Rip's son and heir, who was the ditto of himself, seen leaning against the tree, he was employed to work on the farm, but evinced a hereditary disposition to attend to anything else but his business.

Rip now resumed his old walks and habits; he soon found many of his former cronies, though all rather the worse for the wear and tear of time, and preferred making friends among the rising generation, with whom he soon grew into great favor.

Having nothing to do at home, and being arrived at that happy age when a man can be idle with impunity, he took his place once more on the bench at the inn door and was reverenced as one of the patriarchs of the village, and a chronicle of the old times "before the war." It was some time before he could get into the regular track of gossip, or could be made to comprehend the strange events that had taken place during his torpor. How that there had been a revolutionary war—that the country had thrown off the yoke of old England—and that, instead of being a subject of his Majesty George the Third, he was now a free citizen of the United States. Rip, in fact, was no politician—the changes of states and empires made but little impression on him; but there was one species of despotism under which he had long groaned, and that was—petticoat government. Happily that was at an end; he had got his neck out of the yoke of matrimony and could go in and out whenever he pleased, without dreading the tyranny of Dame Van Winkle. Whenever her name was mentioned, however, he shook his head, shrugged his shoulders, and cast up his eyes, which might pass either for an expression of resignation to his fate or joy at his deliverance.

He used to tell his story to every stranger that arrived at Mr. Doolittle's hotel. He was observed, at first, to vary on some points every time he told it, which was, doubtless, owing to his having so recently awaked. It at last settled down precisely to the tale I have related, and not a man, woman, or child in the neighborhood but knew it by heart. Some always pretended to doubt the reality of it, and insisted that Rip had been out of his head, and that this was one point on which he always remained flighty. The old Dutch inhabitants, however, almost universally gave it full credit. Even to this day they never hear a thunderstorm of a summer afternoon about the Kaatskill but they say Hendrick Hudson and his crew are at their game of ninepins; and it is a common wish of all henpecked husbands in the neighborhood, when life hangs heavy on their hands, that they might have a quieting draft out of Rip Van Winkle's flagon.

THE WRECK

From The Swiss Family Robinson
By Johann David Wyss

This is an abridged version of the introductory chapter of this classic story, adapted for young readers. The abridgement which shows that the device is not new was made in the year 1888 and is also interesting because only one syllable words are used.

WHEN ONE HAS a good tale to tell, he should try to be brief, and not say more than he can help ere he makes a fair start; so I shall not say a word of what took place on board the ship till we had been six days in a storm. The bark had gone far out of her true course, and no one on board knew where we were. The masts lay in splints on the deck, the sails were torn, a leak in the side of the ship let more in than the crew could pump out, and each one felt that ere long he would find a grave in the deep sea, which rose and fell in great white waves of foam, and sent its spray from side to side of what was now but a mere hulk.

Most of those on board sought the best means they could think of to save their own lives; but some knelt down to pray that God would quell the storm and still the waves, for they felt that none but He could help them now.

"Come, boys," said I to my four sons, who were with me, and were struck dumb with fear, "God can save us if it please Him so to do; but, if this is to be our last hour, let us bow to His will—we shall at least all go down side by side."

My dear wife could not hide the tears that fell down her cheeks as I thus spoke to my sons, but she was calm, and knelt down to pray, while the boys clung round her as if they thought she could help them.

Just then we heard a cry of "Land! land!" felt a shock, and were thrown down upon the deck. It was clear that we had struck on a rock, for we heard a loud cry from one of the men, "We are lost! Launch the boat; try for your lives!" These words went, as it were, through my heart like a knife; but, as I felt that I ought to cheer my sons, I said to them, "Now is the time to show that we are brave; we still have life, the land is near, and we know that God helps those who trust in Him. Keep up your hearts, then, while I go and see if there be not some hope yet left for us."

I went at once on deck, and was met by a wave that threw me down, and wet me through to the skin. When I got up, and went to the side of the ship, I found that all the boats had been let down, and that the last of the crew had just left it. I cried out for the men to come back and take us with them, but it was in vain, for the sound of my voice did not reach them through the roar of the waves.

I then thought that our last chance was gone. Still, as I felt that the ship did not sink, I went to the stern, and found, to my joy, that she was held up by a piece of rock on each side, and made fast like a wedge. At the same time I saw some trace of land, which lay to the south, and this made me go back with some hope that we had still a faint chance, though how to get from the ship I could not tell.

As soon as I got downstairs I took my wife by the hand, and said, "Be of good cheer, we are at least safe for some time, and if the wind should veer round, we may yet reach the land that lies but a short way off."

I said this to calm the fears of my wife and sons, and it did so far more than I had a right to hope.

"Let us now take some food," said my wife. "We are sure to need it, for this will no doubt be a night to try our strength."

We still heard the roar of the sea, and now and then the planks would creak as if they were torn up from the deck, so that we had still good cause to fear that we might go down.

My wife got some food for her boys, which we were glad to see them eat, poor as it was; but we could not share their meal. Three out of the four were put to bed in their berths, and soon went to sleep; but Fritz, who was our first child, would not leave us. He said, like a good son, that he would try to be of some use, and think what could be done.

"If we could but find some cork," said Fritz to me in a low tone, "we might make floats. You and I will not need them, for we can swim, but the rest will want some such means to keep them up, and then we can help them to reach the land."

"A good thought," said I. "Let us try in the night to find what things there are in the ship that we can thus make use of."

We soon found some casks and ropes, and with these we made a kind of float for each of the three boys, and then my wife made one for her own use. This done, we got some knives, string, and such things as we could make fast to our belts. We did not fail to look for and find a flint and steel, and the box in which the burnt rags were kept, for these were at that time in use as the means to strike a light.

Fritz, who was now well nigh worn out, laid down on his bed, and slept like the rest. As for me and my poor wife, we kept watch, each in fear lest the next wave should lift the ship off the rock and break it up. We spent part of the night in thought as to our plans for the next day, and sought God to bless the means we had in view to save our lives.

I need not tell you how glad we were when we saw the first gleam of light shine through the chink of the door that shut us in from the cold night air. At dawn the wind did not blow so strong, the sky was clear of clouds, and we saw the sun rise, and with it rose our hopes. I soon had my wife and sons on deck. The boys did not know till then that all the men had left the ship, and that there was no one but us on board.

"Where are the men?" said they. "How can we steer the ship?"

"My dear boys," said I, "He who has kept us safe till now will still aid us, if we do not give way to fear. Let all hands set to work, and leave the rest to God."

At these words we all went to work with a will. My wife went to feed the live stock; Fritz set off in search of arms, and the means to make use of them; and Ernest made his way to the tool chest. Jack ran to pick up what he could find, but as he got to one of the doors he gave it a push, and two huge dogs sprang out and leapt at him. He thought at first they would bite him, but he soon found that they meant him no harm, and one of them let him get on his back and ride up to me as I came from the hold of the ship. I could not keep back a smile, but I told him that it was not safe thus to play with dogs which had not been fed for so long a time.

When the boys had done their search, and the spoil was

brought on deck, we thought we had found all that we should need. "As for me," said my wife, "I have brought good news, for I find we have still on board a cow, an ass, two goats, six sheep, a ram, a pig, and a sow, and I have found food for them all."

"All that you bring will be of use," said I; "but I fear that Jack's dogs will do us more harm than good."

"Not at all," said Jack, in his pert way, "for they can help us to hunt when we get to land."

"Well said, Jack. And now let us see what we can do that will aid us to get there."

We then took the casks that we had found, and as both Ernest and I could use the saw, we soon cut them in half. With these tubs, which were bound round with strong hoops, we made a kind of raft, though it was no slight task. The tubs, in fact, were a fleet of eight small round boats, made so fast to some planks that no one of them could float from the rest. When we had done this, we sat down to a good meal, which we ate with great zest, for we now felt that we had done our best to earn it.

The next thing to be done was to launch the raft. This we at length did, and when the boys saw it slide down the side of the ship and float on the sea, they gave a loud shout, and each one tried who should be the first to get on it. I made it fast to the ship, and there left it.

It was late ere our work was thus far brought to an end; and, as we had to spend at least one night more on the wreck, I told the boys to get a good night's rest, so that they might be fresh for the toils of the next day.

I then told my wife to change her dress for that of one of the crew which she had found, as her skirts would have got in her way when she had to climb. She did not at first like this, but did so as soon as she saw the truth of what I told her.

At last, when all was done, we went to bed, and slept as sound as if we had been on land.

THE DUCK AND THE KANGAROO

I

Said the Duck to the Kangaroo,
  "Good gracious! how you hop
Over the fields, and the water too,
  As if you never would stop!
My life is a bore in this nasty pond;
And I long to go out in the world beyond:
  I wish I could hop like you,"
  Said the Duck to the Kangaroo.

II

"Please give me a ride on your back,"
  Said the Duck to the Kangaroo:
"I would sit quite still, and say nothing but 'Quack'
  The whole of the long day through;

And we'd go the Dee, and the Jelly Bo Lee,
Over the land, and over the sea:
  Please take me a ride! oh, do!"
  Said the Duck to the Kangaroo.

III

Said the Kangaroo to the Duck,
  "This requires some little reflection.
Perhaps, on the whole, it might bring me luck:
  And there seems but one objection;
Which is, if you'll let me speak so bold,
Your feet are unpleasantly wet and cold,
  And would probably give me the roo-
  Matiz," said the Kangaroo.

IV

Said the Duck, "As I sate on the rocks,
  I have thought over that completely;
And I bought four pairs of worsted socks,
  Which fit my web-feet neatly;
And, to keep out the cold, I've bought a cloak;
And every day a cigar I'll smoke;
  All to follow my own dear true
  Love of a Kangaroo."

V

Said the Kangaroo, "I'm ready,
  All in the moonlight pale;
But to balance me well, dear Duck, sit steady,
  And quite at the end of my tail."
So away they went with a hop and a bound;
And they hopped the whole world three times round.
  And who so happy, oh! who,
  As the Duck and the Kangaroo?

Edward Lear

THE RIVER BANK

From The Wind In The Willows
By Kenneth Grahame

THE MOLE had been working very hard all the morning, spring-cleaning his little home. First with brooms, then with dusters; then on ladders and steps and chairs, with a brush and a pail of whitewash; till he had dust in his throat and eyes, and splashes of whitewash all over his black fur, and an aching back and weary arms. Spring was moving in the air above and in the earth below and around him, penetrating even his dark and lowly little house with its spirit of divine discontent and longing. It was small wonder, then, that he suddenly flung down his brush on the floor, said "Bother!" and "O blow!" and also "Hang spring-cleaning!" and bolted out of the house without even waiting to put on his coat. Something up above was calling him imperiously, and he made for the steep little tunnel which answered in his case to the gravelled carriage-drive owned by animals whose residences are nearer to the sun and air. So he scraped and scratched and scrabbled and scrooged, and then he scrooged again and scrabbled and scratched and scraped, working busily with his little paws and muttering to himself, "Up we go! Up we go!" till at last, pop! his snout came out into the sunlight, and he found himself rolling in the warm grass of a great meadow.

"This is fine!" he said to himself. "This is better than whitewashing!" The sunshine struck hot on his fur, soft breezes caressed his heated brow, and after the seclusion of the cellarage he had lived in so long the carol of happy birds fell on his dulled hearing almost like a shout. Jumping off all his four legs at once, in the joy of living and the delight of spring without its cleaning, he pursued his way across the meadow till he reached the hedge on the further side.

"Hold up!" said an elderly rabbit at the gap. "Sixpence for the privilege of passing by the private road!" He was bowled over in an instant by the impatient and contemptuous Mole, who trotted along the side of the hedge chaffing the other rabbits as they peeped hurriedly from their holes to see what the row was about. "Onion-sauce! Onion-sauce!" he remarked jeeringly, and was gone before they could think of a thoroughly satisfactory reply. Then they all started grumbling at each

other. "How *stupid* you are! Why didn't you tell him—" "Well, why didn't *you* say—" "You might have reminded him—" and so on, in the usual way; but, of course, it was then much too late, as is always the case.

It all seemed too good to be true. Hither and thither through the meadows he rambled busily, along the hedgerows, across the copses, finding everywhere birds building, flowers budding, leaves thrusting—everything happy, and progressive, and occupied. And instead of having an uneasy conscience pricking him and whispering "Whitewash!" he somehow could only feel how jolly it was to be the only idle dog among all these busy citizens. After all, the best part of a holiday is perhaps not so much to be resting yourself, as to see all the other fellows busy working.

He thought his happiness was complete when, as he meandered aimlessly along, suddenly he stood by the edge of a full-fed river. Never in his life had he seen a river before—this sleek, sinuous, full-bodied animal, chasing and chuckling, gripping things with a gurgle and leaving them with a laugh, to fling itself on fresh playmates that shook themselves free, and were caught and held again. All was a-shake and a-shiver—glints and gleams and sparkles, rustle and swirl, chatter and bubble. The Mole was bewitched, entranced, fascinated. By the side of the river he trotted as one trots, when very small, by the side of a man who holds one spellbound by exciting stories; and when tired at last, he sat on the bank, while the river still chattered on to him, a babbling procession of the best stories in the world, sent from the heart of the earth to be told at last to the insatiable sea.

As he sat on the grass and looked across the river, a dark hole in the bank opposite, just above the water's edge, caught his eye, and dreamily he fell to considering what a nice snug dwelling-place it would make for an animal with few wants and fond of a bijou riverside residence, above flood level and remote from noise and dust. As he gazed, something bright and small seemed to twinkle down in the heart of it, vanished, then

twinkled once more like a tiny star. But it could hardly be a star in such an unlikely situation; and it was too glittering and small for a glow-worm. Then, as he looked, it winked at him, and so declared itself to be an eye; and a small face began gradually to grow up round it, like a frame round a picture.

A brown little face, with whiskers.

A grave round face, with the same twinkle in its eye that had first attracted his notice.

Small neat ears and thick silky hair.

It was the Water Rat!

Then the two animals stood and regarded each other cautiously.

"Hullo, Mole!" said the Water Rat.

"Hullo, Rat!" said the Mole.

"Would you like to come over?" inquired the Rat presently.

"Oh, it's all very well to *talk*," said the Mole rather pettishly, he being new to a river and riverside life and its ways.

The Rat said nothing, but stooped and unfastened a rope and hauled on it; then lightly stepped into a little boat which the Mole had not observed. It was painted blue outside and white within, and was just the size for two animals; and the Mole's whole heart went out to it at once, even though he did not yet fully understand its uses.

The Rat sculled smartly across and made fast. Then he held up his fore-paw as the Mole stepped gingerly down. "Lean on that!" he said. "Now then, step lively!" and the Mole to his surprise and rapture found himself actually seated in the stern of a real boat.

"This has been a wonderful day!" said he, as the Rat

shoved off and took to the sculls again. "Do you know, I've never been in a boat before in all my life."

"What?" cried the Rat, open-mouthed: "Never been in a—you never—well, I—what have you been doing, then?"

"Is it so nice as all that?" asked the Mole shyly, though he was quite prepared to believe it as he leant back in his seat and surveyed the cushions, the oars, the row-locks, and all the fascinating fittings, and felt the boat sway lightly under him.

"Nice? It's the *only* thing," said the Water Rat solemnly, as he leant forward for his stroke. "Believe me, my young friend, there is *nothing*—absolutely nothing—half so much worth doing as simply messing about in boats. Simply messing," he went on dreamily: "messing—about—in—boats; messing—"

"Look ahead, Rat!" cried the Mole suddenly.

It was too late. The boat struck the bank full tilt. The dreamer, the joyous oarsman, lay on his back at the bottom of the boat, his heels in the air.

"—about in boats—or *with* boats," the Rat went on composedly, picking himself up with a pleasant laugh. "In or out of 'em, it doesn't matter. Nothing seems really to matter, that's the charm of it. Whether you get away, or whether you don't; whether you arrive at your destination or whether you reach somewhere else, or whether you never get anywhere at all, you're always busy, and you never do anything in particular; and when you've done it there's always something else to do, and you can do it if you like, but you'd much better not. Look here! If you've really nothing else on hand this morning, supposing we drop down the river together, and have a long day of it?"

The Mole waggled his toes from sheer happiness, spread his chest with a sigh of full contentment, and leaned back blissfully into the soft cushions. "*What* a day I'm having!" he said. "Let us start at once!"

"Hold hard a minute, then!" said the Rat. He looped the painter through a ring in his landing-stage, climbed up into his hole above, and after a short interval reappeared staggering under a fat, wicker luncheon-basket.

"Shove that under your feet," he observed to the Mole, as he passed it down into the boat. Then he untied the painter and took the sculls again.

"What's inside it?" asked the Mole, wiggling with curiosity.

"There's cold chicken inside it," replied the Rat briefly; "coldtonguecoldhamcoldbeefpickledgherkinssaladfrenchrolls-cressandwidgespottedmeatgingerbeerlemonadesodawater—"

"O stop, stop," cried the Mole in ecstasies: "This is too much!"

"Do you really think so?" inquired the Rat seriously. "It's only what I always take on these little excursions; and the other animals are always telling me that I'm a mean beast and cut it *very* fine!"

The Mole never heard a word he was saying. Absorbed in the new life he was entering upon, intoxicated with the sparkle, the ripple, the scents and the sounds and the sunlight, he trailed a paw in the water and dreamed long waking dreams. The Water Rat, like the good little fellow he was, sculled steadily on and forbore to disturb him.

"I like your clothes awfully, old chap," he remarked after some half an hour or so had passed. "I'm going to get a black velvet smoking suit myself some day, as soon as I can afford it."

"I beg your pardon," said the Mole, pulling himself together with an effort. "You must think me very rude; but all this is so new to me. So—this—is—a—River!"

"*The* River," corrected the Rat.

"And you really live by the river? What a jolly life!"

"By it and with it and on it and in it," said the Rat. "It's brother and sister to me, and aunts, and company, and food and drink, and (naturally) washing. It's my world, and I don't want any other. What it hasn't got is not worth having, and what it doesn't know is not worth knowing. Lord! the times we've had together! Whether in winter or summer, spring or autumn, it's always got its fun and its excitements. When the floods are on in February, and my cellars and basement are brimming with drink that's no good to me, and the brown water runs by my best bedroom window; or again when it all drops away and shows patches of mud that smells like plum-cake, and the rushes and weed clog the channels, and I can potter about dry-shod over most of the bed of it and find fresh food to eat, and things careless people have dropped out of boats!"

"But isn't it a bit dull at times?" the Mole ventured to ask. "Just you and the river, and no one else to pass a word with?"

"No one else to—well, I mustn't be hard on you," said the Rat with forbearance. "You're new to it, and of course you don't know. The bank is so crowded nowadays that many people are moving away altogether. O no, it isn't what it used to be, at all. Otters, kingfishers, dabchicks, moorhens, all of them about all day long and always wanting you to *do* something—as if a fellow had no business of his own to attend to!"

"What lies over *there?*" asked the Mole, waving a paw towards a background of woodland that darkly framed the water-meadows on one side of the river.

"That? O, that's just the Wild Wood," said the Rat shortly. "We don't go there very much, we river-bankers."

"Aren't they—aren't they very *nice* people in there?" said the Mole a trifle nervously.

"W-e-ll," replied the Rat, "let me see. The squirrels are all right. *And* the rabbits—some of 'em, but rabbits are a mixed lot. And then there's Badger, of course. He lives right in the heart of it; wouldn't live anywhere else, either, if you paid him to do it. Dear old Badger! Nobody interferes with *him*. They'd better not," he added significantly.

"Why, who *should* interfere with him?" asked the Mole.

"Well, of course—there—are others," explained the Rat in a hesitating sort of way. "Weasels—and stoats—and foxes—and so on. They're all right in a way—I'm very good friends with them—pass the time of day when we meet, and all that—but they break out sometimes, there's no denying it, and then—well, you can't really trust them, and that's the fact."

The Mole knew well that it is quite against animal-etiquette to dwell on possible trouble ahead, or even to allude to it; so he dropped the subject.

"And beyond the Wild Wood again?" he asked: "Where it's all blue and dim, and one sees what may be hills or perhaps they mayn't, and something like the smoke of towns, or is it only cloud-drift?"

"Beyond the Wild Wood comes the Wide World," said the Rat. "And that's something that doesn't matter, either to you or me. I've never been there, and I'm never going, nor you either, if you've got any sense at all. Don't ever refer to it again, please. Now then! Here's our backwater at last, where we're going to lunch."

Leaving the main stream, they now passed into what seemed at first sight like a little land-locked lake. Green turf sloped down to either edge, brown snaky tree-roots gleamed below the surface of the quiet water, while ahead of them the silvery shoulder and foamy tumble of a weir, arm-in-arm with a restless dripping mill-wheel, that held up in its turn a grey-gabled mill-house, filled the air with a soothing murmur of sound, dull and smothery, yet with little clear voices speaking up cheerfully out of it at intervals. It was so very beautiful that the Mole could only hold up both fore-paws and gasp, "O my! O my! O my!"

The Rat brought the boat alongside the bank, made her fast, helped the still awkward Mole safely ashore, and swung out the luncheon-basket.

The Mole begged as a favour to be allowed to unpack it all by himself; and the Rat was very pleased to indulge him,

and to sprawl at full length on the grass and rest, while his excited friend shook out the tablecloth and spread it, took out all the mysterious packets one by one and arranged their contents in due order, still gasping, "O my! O my!" at each fresh revelation. When all was ready, the Rat said, "Now, pitch in, old fellow!" and the Mole was indeed very glad to obey, for he had started his spring-cleaning at a very early hour that morning, as people *will* do, and had not paused for bite or sup; and he had been through a very great deal since that distant time which now seemed so many days ago.

"What are you looking at?" said the Rat presently, when the edge of their hunger was somewhat dulled, and the Mole's eyes were able to wander off the tablecloth a little.

"I am looking," said the Mole, "at a streak of bubbles that I see traveling along the surface of the water. That is a thing that strikes me as funny."

"Bubbles? Oho!" said the Rat, and chirruped cheerily in an inviting sort of way.

A broad glistening muzzle showed itself above the edge of the bank, and the Otter hauled himself out and shook the water from his coat.

"Greedy beggars!" he observed, making for the provender. "Why didn't you invite me, Ratty?"

"This was an impromptu affair," explained the Rat. "By the way—my friend Mr. Mole."

"Proud, I'm sure," said the Otter, and the two animals were friends forthwith.

"Such a rumpus everywhere!" continued the Otter. "All the world seems out on the river to-day. I came up this backwater to try and get a moment's peace, and then stumble upon you fellows!—At least—I beg pardon—I don't exactly mean that, you know."

There was a rustle behind them, proceeding from a

hedge wherein last year's leaves still clung thick, and a stripy head, with high shoulders behind it, peered forth on them.

"Come on, old Badger," shouted the Rat.

The Badger trotted forward a pace or two; then grunted, "H'm! Company," and turned his back and disappeared from view.

"That's *just* the sort of fellow he is!" observed the disappointed Rat. "Simply hates Society! Now we shan't see any more of him today. Well, tell us *who's* out on the river?"

"Toad's out, for one," replied the Otter. "In his brand-new wager-boat; new togs, new everything!"

The two animals looked at each other and laughed.

"Once, it was nothing but sailing," said the Rat. "Then he tired of that and took to punting. Nothing would please him but to punt all day and every day, and a nice mess he made of it. Last year it was house-boating, and we all had to go and stay with him in his house-boat, and pretend we liked it. He was going to spend the rest of his life in a house-boat. It's all the same whatever he takes up; he gets tired of it, and starts on something fresh."

"Such a good fellow, too," remarked the Otter reflectively: "But no stability—especially in a boat!"

From where they sat they could get a glimpse of the main stream across the island that separated them; and just then a wager-boat flashed into view, the rower—a short, stout figure—splashing badly and rolling a good deal, but working his hardest. The Rat stood up and hailed him, but Toad—for it was he—shook his head and settled sternly to his work.

"He'll be out of the boat in a minute if he rolls like that," said the Rat, sitting down again.

"Of course he will," chuckled the Otter. "Did I ever tell you that good story about Toad and the lock-keeper? It happened this way. Toad . . ."

An errant May-fly swerved unsteadily athwart the current in the intoxicated fashion affected by young bloods of May-flies seeing life. A swirl of water and a "cloop!" and the May-fly was visible no more.

Neither was the Otter.

The Mole looked down. The voice was still in his ears, but the turf whereon he had sprawled was clearly vacant. Not an Otter to be seen, as far as the distant horizon.

But again there was a streak of bubbles on the surface of the river.

The Rat hummed a tune, and the Mole recollected that animal-etiquette forbade any sort of comment on the sudden disappearance of one's friends at any moment, for any reason or no reason whatever.

"Well, well," said the Rat, "I suppose we ought to be moving. I wonder which of us had better pack the luncheon-basket?" He did not speak as if he was frightfully eager for the treat.

"O, please let me," said the Mole. So, of course, the Rat let him.

Packing the basket was not quite such pleasant work as unpacking the basket. It never is. But the Mole was bent on enjoying everything, and although just when he had got the basket packed and strapped up tightly he saw a plate staring up at him from the grass, and when the job had been done again the Rat pointed out a fork which anybody ought to have seen, and last of all, behold! the mustard pot, which he had been sitting on without knowing it—still, somehow, the thing got finished at last, without much loss of temper.

The afternoon sun was getting low as the Rat sculled gently homewards in a dreamy mood, murmuring poetry-things over to himself, and not paying much attention to Mole. But the Mole was very full of lunch, and self-satisfaction, and pride, and already quite at home in a boat (so he thought) and was getting a bit restless besides: and presently he said, "Ratty! Please, *I* want to row, now!"

The Rat shook his head with a smile. "Not yet, my young friend," he said—"wait till you've had a few lessons. It's not so easy as it looks."

The Mole was quiet for a minute or two. But he began to feel more and more jealous of Rat, sculling so strongly and so easily along, and his pride began to whisper that he could do it every bit as well. He jumped up and seized the sculls so suddenly, that the Rat, who was gazing out over the water and saying more poetry-things to himself, was taken by surprise and fell backwards off his seat with his legs in the air for the second time, while the triumphant Mole took his place and grabbed the sculls with entire confidence.

"Stop it, you *silly* ass!" cried the Rat, from the bottom of the boat. "You can't do it! You'll have us over!"

The Mole flung his sculls back with a flourish, and made a great dig at the water. He missed the surface altogether, his legs flew up above his head, and he found himself lying on the top of the prostrate Rat. Greatly alarmed, he made a grab at the side of the boat, and the next moment—Sploosh!

Over went the boat, and he found himself struggling in the river.

O my, how cold the water was, and O, how *very* wet it

felt. How it sang in his ears as he went down, down, down! How bright and welcome the sun looked as he rose to the surface coughing and spluttering! How black was his despair when he felt himself sinking again! Then a firm paw gripped him by the back of his neck. It was the Rat, and he was evidently laughing—the Mole could *feel* him laughing, right down his arm and through his paw, and so into his—the Mole's—neck.

The Rat got hold of a scull and shoved it under the Mole's arm; then he did the same by the other side of him and, swimming behind, propelled the helpless animal to shore, hauled him out, and set him down on the bank, a squashy, pulpy lump of misery.

When the Rat had rubbed him down a bit, and wrung some of the wet out of him, he said, "Now, then, old fellow! Trot up and down the towing-path as hard as you can, till you're warm and dry again, while I dive for the luncheon-basket."

So the dismal Mole, wet without and ashamed within, trotted about till he was fairly dry, while the Rat plunged into the water again, recovered the boat, righted her and made her fast, fetched his floating property to shore by degrees, and finally dived successfully for the luncheon-basket and struggled to land with it.

When all was ready for a start once more, the Mole, limp and dejected, took his seat in the stern of the boat; and as they set off, he said in a low voice, broken with emotion, "Ratty, my generous friend! I am very sorry indeed for my foolish and ungrateful conduct. My heart quite fails me when I think how I might have lost that beautiful luncheon-basket. Indeed, I have been a complete ass, and I know it. Will you overlook it this once and forgive me, and let things go on as before?"

"That's all right, bless you!" responded the Rat cheerily. "What's a little wet to a Water Rat? I'm more in the water than out of it most days. Don't you think any more about it; and, look here! I really think you had better come and stop with me for a little time. It's very plain and rough, you know—not like Toad's house at all—but you haven't seen that yet;

still, I can make you comfortable. And I'll teach you to row, and to swim, and you'll soon be as handy on the water as any of us."

The Mole was so touched by his kind manner of speaking that he could find no voice to answer him; and he had to brush away a tear or two with the back of his paw. But the Rat kindly looked in another direction, and presently the Mole's spirits revived again, and he was even able to give some straight back-talk to a couple of moorhens who were sniggering to each other about his bedraggled appearance.

When they got home, the Rat made a bright fire in the parlour, and planted the Mole in an arm-chair in front of it, having fetched down a dressing-gown and slippers for him, and told him river stories till supper-time. Very thrilling stories they were, too, to an earth-dwelling animal like Mole. Stories about weirs, and sudden floods, and leaping pike, and steamers that flung hard bottles—at least bottles were certainly

flung, and *from* steamers, so presumably *by* them; and about herons, and how particular they were whom they spoke to; and about adventures down drains, and night-fishings with Otter, or excursions far afield with Badger. Supper was a most cheerful meal; but very shortly afterwards a terribly sleepy Mole had to be escorted upstairs by his considerate host, to the best bedroom, where he soon laid his head on his pillow in great peace and contentment, knowing that his new-found friend the River was lapping the sill of his window.

This day was only the first of many similar ones for the emancipated Mole, each of them longer and fuller of interest as the ripening summer moved onward. He learnt to swim and to row, and entered into the joy of running water; and with his ear to the reed-stems he caught, at intervals, something of what the wind went whispering so constantly among them.

TOM BECOMES A WATER BABY

From The Water Babies
By Charles Kingsley

Tom, the chimney-sweep, has fled Harthover Place, pursued by Sir John and Tom's master, the wretched Mr. Grimes. While sweeping chimneys at Harthover Place, Tom loses his way inside the large, crooked flues and by accident enters the bedroom of Sir John's sleeping daughter whose screams arouse the entire household. Tom outruns his pursuers but always close to him is a beautiful Irishwoman whom Tom never sees. We now come upon the tired, hungry Tom, climbing down a precipitous mountain as he tries to reach a cottage far, far below where he has spied a little woman in a red petticoat walking in her garden.

A MILE OFF and a thousand feet down.

So Tom found it; though it seemed as if he could have chucked a pebble on to the back of the woman in the red petticoat who was weeding in the garden, or even across the dale to the rocks beyond. For the bottom of the valley was just one field broad, and on the other side ran the stream; and above it, grey crag, grey down, grey stair, grey moor walled up to heaven.

A quiet, silent, rich, happy place; a narrow crack cut deep into the earth; so deep, and so out of the way, that the bad bogies can hardly find it out. The name of the place is Vendale.

So Tom went to go down; and first he went down three hundred feet of steep heather, mixed up with loose brown gritstone, as rough as a file; which was not pleasant to his poor little heels, as he came bump, stump, jump, down the steep. And still he thought he could throw a stone into the garden.

Then he went down three hundred feet of limestone terraces, one below the other, as straight as if a carpenter had ruled them with his ruler and then cut them out with his chisel. There was no heath there, but—

First, a little grass slope, covered with the prettiest flowers, rockrose and saxifrage, and thyme and basil, and all sorts of sweet herbs.

Then bump down a two-foot step of limestone.

Then another bit of grass and flowers.

Then bump down a one-foot step.

Then another bit of grass and flowers for fifty yards, as steep as the house-roof, where he had to slide down on his dear little tail.

Then another step of stone, ten feet high; and there he had to stop himself, and crawl along the edge to find a crack; for if he had rolled over, he would have rolled right into the old woman's garden, and frightened her out of her wits.

Then, when he had found a dark narrow crack, full of green-stalked fern, such as hangs in the basket in the drawing-room, and had crawled down through it, with knees and elbows, as he would down a chimney, there was another grass slope, and another step, and so on, till—oh, dear me! I wish it was all over; and so did he. And yet he thought he could throw a stone into the old woman's garden.

At last he came to a bank of beautiful shrubs; white-beam with its great silver-backed leaves, and mountain-ash, and oak; and below them cliff and crag, cliff and crag, with great beds of crown-ferns and wood-sedge; while through the shrubs he could see the stream sparkling, and hear it murmur on the white pebbles. He did not know that it was three hundred feet below.

You would have been giddy, perhaps, at looking down: but Tom was not. He was a brave little chimney-sweep; and when he found himself on the top of a high cliff, instead of sitting down and crying for his baba (though he never had had any baba to cry for), he said, "Ah, this will just suit me!" though he was very tired; and down he went, by stock and stone, sedge and ledge, bush and rush, as if he had been born a jolly little black ape, with four hands instead of two.

And all the while he never saw the Irishwoman coming down behind him.

But he was getting terribly tired now. The burning sun on the fells had sucked him up; but the damp heat of the woody crag sucked him up still more; and the perspiration ran out of the ends of his fingers and toes, and washed him cleaner than he had been for a whole year. But, of course, he dirtied everything terribly as he went. There has been a great black smudge all down the crag ever since. And there have been more black beetles in Vendale since than ever were known before; all, of course, owing to Tom's having blacked the original papa of them all, just as he was setting off to be married, with a sky-blue coat and scarlet leggings, as smart as a gardener's dog with a polyanthus in his mouth.

At last he got to the bottom. But, behold, it was not the bottom—as people usually find when they are coming down a mountain. For at the foot of the crag were heaps and heaps of fallen limestone of every size from that of your head to that of a stage-waggon, with holes between them full of sweet heath-fern; and before Tom got through them, he was out in the bright sunshine again; and then he felt, once for all and suddenly, as people generally do, that he was b-e-a-t, beat.

He could not get on. The sun was burning, and yet he felt chill all over. He was quite empty, and yet he felt quite sick. There was but two hundred yards of smooth pasture between him and the cottage, and yet he could not walk down it. He could hear the stream murmuring only one field

beyond it, and yet it seemed to him as if it was a hundred miles off.

He lay down on the grass till the beetles ran over him, and the flies settled on his nose. I don't know when he would have got up again, if the gnats and the midges had not taken compassion on him. But the gnats blew their trumpets so loud in his ear, and midges nibbled so at his hands and face wherever they could find a place free from soot, that at last he woke up, and stumbled away, down over a low wall, and into a narrow road, and up to the cottage door.

And a neat pretty cottage it was, with clipt yew hedges all round the garden, and yews inside too, cut into peacocks and trumpets and teapots and all kinds of queer shapes. And out of the open door came a noise like that of the frogs on the Great-A, when they know that it is going to be scorching hot to-morrow—and how they know that I don't know, and you don't know, and nobody knows.

He came slowly up to the open door, which was all hung round with clematis and roses; and then peeped in, half afraid.

And there sat by the empty fireplace, which was filled with a pot of sweet herbs, the nicest old woman that ever was seen, in her red petticoat, and short dimity bedgown, and clean white cap, with a black silk handkerchief over it, tied under her chin. At her feet sat the grandfather of all the cats; and opposite her sat, on two benches, twelve or fourteen neat, rosy, chubby little children, learning their Chris-cros row; and gabble enough they made about it. Such a pleasant cottage it was, with a shiny clean stone floor, and curious old prints on the walls, and an old black sideboard oak full of bright pewter and brass dishes, and a cuckoo-clock in the corner, which began shouting as soon as Tom appeared: not that it was frightened at Tom, but that it was just eleven o'clock.

All the children started at Tom's dirty black figure—the girls began to cry, and the boys began to laugh, and all

pointed at him rudely enough; but Tom was too tired to care for that.

"What art thou, and what dost want?" cried the old dame. "A chimney-sweep! Away with thee! I'll have no sweeps here."

"Water," said poor Tom, quite faint.

"Water? There's plenty i' the beck," she said, quite sharply.

"But I can't get there; I'm most clemmed with hunger and drought." And Tom sank down upon the door-step, and laid his head against the post.

And the old dame looked at him through her spectacles one minute, and two, and three; and then she said, "He's sick, and a bairn's a bairn, sweep or none."

"Water," said Tom.

"God forgive me!" and she put by her spectacles, and rose, and came to Tom. "Water's bad for thee; I'll give thee milk." And she toddled off into the next room, and brought a cup of milk and a bit of bread.

Tom drank the milk off at one draught, and then looked up, revived.

"Where didst come from?" said the dame.

"Over Fell, there," said Tom, and pointed up into the sky.

"Over Harthover? and down Lewthwaite Crag? Art sure thou art not lying?"

"Why should I?" said Tom, and leant his head against the post.

"And how got ye up there?"

"I came over from the Place;" and Tom was so tired and desperate he had no heart or time to think of a story, so he told all the truth in a few words.

"Bless thy little heart! And thou hast not been stealing, then?"

"No."

"Bless thy little heart! and I'll warrant not. Why, God's guided the bairn, because he was innocent! Away from the Place, and over Harthover Fell, and down Lewthwaite Crag! Who ever heard the like, if God hadn't led him? Why dost not eat thy bread?"

"I can't."

"It's good enough, for I made it myself."

"I can't," said Tom, and he laid his head on his knees, and then asked—

"Is it Sunday?"

"No, then; why should it be?"

"Because I hear the church-bells ringing so."

"Bless thy pretty heart! The bairn's sick. Come wi' me, and I'll hap thee up somewhere. If thou wert a bit cleaner I'd put thee in my own bed, for the Lord's sake. But come along here."

But when Tom tried to get up, he was so tired and giddy that she had to help him and lead him.

She put him in an outhouse upon soft sweet hay and an old rug, and bade him sleep off his walk, and she would come to him when school was over, in an hour's time.

And so she went in again, expecting Tom to fall fast asleep at once.

But Tom did not fall asleep.

Instead of it he turned and tossed and kicked about in the strangest way, and felt so hot all over that he longed to get into the river and cool himself; and then he fell half asleep, and dreamt that he heard the little white lady crying to him, "Oh, you're so dirty; go and be washed"; and then that he heard the Irishwoman saying, "Those that wish to be clean, clean they will be." And then he heard the church-bells ring so loud, close to him too, that he was sure it must be Sunday, in spite of what the old dame had said; and he would go to church, and see what a church was like inside, for he had never been in one, poor little fellow, in all his life. But the people would never let him come in, all over soot and dirt like that. He must go to the river and wash first. And he said out loud again and again, though being half asleep he did not know it, "I must be clean, I must be clean."

And all of a sudden he found himself, not in the outhouse on the hay, but in the middle of a meadow, over the road, with the stream just before him, saying continually, "I must be clean, I must be clean." He had got there on his own legs, between sleep and awake, as children will often get out of bed, and go about the room, when they are not quite well. But he was not a bit surprised, and went on to the bank of the brook, and lay down on the grass, and looked into the clear, clear limestone water, with every pebble at the bottom bright and clean, while the little silver trout dashed about in fright at the sight of his black face; and he dipped his hand in and found it so cool, cool, cool; and he said, "I will be a fish; I will swim in the water; I must be clean, I must be clean."

So he pulled off all his clothes in such haste that he tore some of them, which was easy enough with such ragged old things. And he put his poor hot sore feet into the water; and then his legs; and the farther he went in, the more the church-bells rang in his head.

"Ah!" said Tom, "I must be quick and wash myself; the bells are ringing quite loud now; and they will stop soon, and then the door will be shut, and I shall never be able to get in at all."

And all the while he never saw the Irishwoman, not behind him this time, but before.

For just before he came to the river-side, she had stepped down into the cool clear water; and her shawl and her petticoat floated off her, and the green waterweeds floated round her sides, and the white water-lilies floated round her head, and the fairies of the stream came up from the bottom and bore her away and down upon their arms; for she was the Queen of them all; and perhaps of more besides.

"Where have you been?" they asked her.

"I have been smoothing sick folk's pillows, and whispering sweet dreams into their ears; opening cottage casements to let out the stifling air; coaxing little children away from the gutters, and foul pools where fever breeds; turning women

from the gin-shop door, and staying men's hands as they were going to strike their wives; doing all I can to help those who will not help themselves: and little enough that is, and weary work for me. But I have brought you a new little brother, and watched him safe all the way here."

Then all the fairies laughed for joy at the thought that they had a little brother coming.

"But mind, maidens, he must not see you, or know that you are here. He is but a savage now, and like the beasts which perish; and from the beasts which perish he must learn. So you must not play with him, or speak to him, or let him see you: but only keep him from being harmed."

Then the fairies were sad, because they could not play with their new brother, but they always did what they were told.

And their Queen floated away down the river; and whither she went, thither she came. But all this Tom, of course, never saw or heard: and perhaps if he had it would have made little difference in the story; for he was so hot and thirsty, and longed so to be clean for once, that he tumbled himself as quick as he could into the clear cool stream.

And he had not been in it two minutes before he fell fast asleep, into the quietest, sunniest, cosiest sleep that ever he had in his life; and he dreamt about the green meadows by which he had walked that morning, and the tall elm-trees, and the sleeping cows; and after that he dreamt of nothing at all.

The reason of his falling into such a delightful sleep is very simple; and yet hardly anyone has found it out. It was merely that the fairies took him.

Ah, now comes the most wonderful part of this wonderful story. Tom, when he woke, for of course he woke—children always wake after they have slept exactly as long as is good for them—found himself swimming about in the stream, being about four inches, or—that I may be accurate—3.87902 inches

long, and having round the parotid region of his fauces a set of external gills (I hope you understand all the big words) just like those of a sucking eft, which he mistook for a lace frill, till he pulled at them, found he hurt himself, and made up his mind that they were part of himself, and best left alone.

In fact, the fairies had turned him into a water-baby.

REEDS OF INNOCENCE

Piping down the valleys wild,
  Piping songs of pleasant glee,
On a cloud I saw a child,
  And he laughing said to me:

"Pipe a song about a Lamb!"
  So I piped with merry cheer.
"Piper, pipe that song again;"
  So I piped: he wept to hear.

"Drop thy pipe, thy happy pipe;
  Sing thy songs of happy cheer!"
So I sung the same again,
  While he wept with joy to hear.

"Piper, sit thee down and write
  In a book that all may read."
So he vanish'd from my sight;
  And I pluck'd a hollow reed,

And I made a rural pen,
  And I stain'd the water clear,
And I wrote my happy songs
  Every child may joy to hear.

William Blake

POEMS

ANIMAL CRACKERS

Animal crackers, and cocoa to drink,
That is the finest of suppers, I think;
When I'm grown up and can have what I please
I think I shall always insist upon these.

What do you choose when you're offered a treat?
When Mother says, "What would you like best to eat?"
Is it waffles and syrup, or cinnamon toast?
It's cocoa and animals that *I* love the most!

The kitchen's the cosiest place that I know:
The kettle is singing, the stove is aglow,
And there in the twilight, how jolly to see
The cocoa and animals waiting for me.

Daddy and Mother dine later in state,
With Mary to cook for them, Susan to wait;
But they don't have nearly as much fun as I
Who eat in the kitchen with Nurse standing by;
And Daddy once said, he would like to be me
Having cocoa and animals once more for tea!

Christopher Morley

THE VILLAGE BLACKSMITH

Under a spreading chestnut tree
  The village smithy stands;
The smith, a mighty man is he,
  With large and sinewy hands;
And the muscles of his brawny arms
  Are strong as iron bands.

His hair is crisp, and black, and long,
  His face is like the tan;
His brow is wet with honest sweat,
  He earns whate'er he can,
And looks the whole world in the face,
  For he owes not any man.

Week in, week out, from morn till night,
  You can hear his bellows blow;
You can hear him swing his heavy sledge,
  With measured beat and slow,
Like a sexton ringing the village bell,
  When the evening sun is low.

And children coming home from school
  Look in at the open door;
They love to see the flaming forge,
  And hear the bellows roar,
And catch the burning sparks that fly
  Like chaff from a threshing-floor.

He goes on Sunday to the church,
  And sits among his boys;
He hears the parson pray and preach,
  He hears his daughter's voice
Singing in the village choir,
  And it makes his heart rejoice.

It sounds to him like her mother's voice,
  Singing in Paradise!
He needs must think of her once more,
  How in the grave she lies;
And with his hard, rough hand he wipes
  A tear out of his eyes.

Toiling—rejoicing—sorrowing,
  Onward through life he goes;
Each morning sees some task begun,
  Each evening sees its close;
Something attempted, something done,
  Has earned a night's repose.

Thanks, thanks to thee, my worthy friend,
  For the lesson thou hast taught!
Thus at the flaming forge of life
  Our fortunes must be wrought;
Thus on its sounding anvil shaped
  Each burning deed and thought!

Henry Wadsworth Longfellow

A TWISTER A-TWISTING

When a Twister a-twisting will twist him a twist;
For the twisting of his twist, he three times doth intwist;
But if one of the twines of the twist do untwist,
The twine that untwisteth, untwisteth the twine.

Untwirling the twine that untwisteth between,
He twirls, with the twister, the two in a twine.
Then twice having twisted the twines of the twine
He twisteth the twine he had twined in twain.

The twain that in twining, before in the twine,
As twines were intwisted; he now doth untwine;
'Twixt the twain inter-twisting a twine more between,
He twirling his twister, makes a twist of the twine.

THE SPIDER AND THE FLY

"Will you walk into my parlour?" said the Spider to the Fly.
" 'Tis the prettiest little parlour that ever you did spy;
The way into my parlour is up a winding stair,
And I have many curious things to show when you are there."
"Oh, no, no," said the little Fly; "to ask me is in vain;
For who goes up your winding stair can ne'er come down
again."
"I'm sure you must be weary, dear, with soaring up so high;
Will you rest upon my little bed?" said the Spider to the Fly.
"There are pretty curtains drawn around; the sheets are fine
and thin,
And if you like to rest awhile, I'll snugly tuck you in!"
"Oh, no, no," said the little Fly, "for I've often heard it said,
They never, never wake again, who sleep upon your bed!"

Said the cunning Spider to the Fly: "Dear friend, what can
I do,
To prove the warm affection I've always felt for you?
I have within my pantry good store of all that's nice;
I'm sure you're very welcome—will you please to take a slice?"
"Oh, no, no," said the little Fly, "kind sir, that cannot be,
I've heard what's in your pantry, and I do not wish to see!"
"Sweet creature!" said the Spider, "you're witty and you're
wise,
How handsome are your gauzy wings, how brilliant are your
eyes;
I have a little looking-glass upon my parlour shelf,
If you'll step in one moment, dear, you shall behold yourself."
"I thank you, gentle sir," she said, "for what you're pleased
to say,
And bidding you good morning now, I call another day."

The Spider turned him round about, and went into his den,
For well he knew the silly Fly would soon come back again:
So he wove a subtle web in a little corner sly,
And set his table ready to dine upon the Fly.

Then he came out to his door again, and merrily did sing,
"Come hither, hither, pretty Fly, with the pearl and silver wing;
Your robes are green and purple—there's a crest upon your head;
Your eyes are like the diamond bright, but mine are dull as lead!"
Alas, alas! how very soon this silly little Fly,
Hearing his wily, flattering words, came slowly flitting by;
With buzzing wings she hung aloft, then near and nearer drew,
Thinking only of her brilliant eyes, and green and purple hue—
Thinking only of her crested head—poor foolish thing!—at last
Up jump'd the cunning Spider, and fiercely held her fast.
He dragg'd her up his winding stair, into his dismal den,
Within his little parlour—but she ne'er came out again!

And now, dear little children, who may this story read,
To idle, silly, flattering words, I pray you ne'er give heed:
Unto an evil counsellor close heart and ear and eye,
And take a lesson from this tale, of the Spider and the Fly.

Mary Howitt

THE RAVEN

Once upon a midnight dreary, while I pondered, weak and
weary,
Over many a quaint and curious volume of forgotten lore—
While I nodded, nearly napping, suddenly there came a
tapping,
As of some one gently rapping, rapping at my chamber door.
" 'T is some visitor," I muttered, "tapping at my chamber
door—
Only this and nothing more."

Ah, distinctly I remember it was in the bleak December;
And each separate dying ember wrought its ghost upon the floor.
Eagerly I wished the morrow;—vainly I had sought to borrow
From my books surcease of sorrow—sorrow for the lost Lenore—
For the rare and radiant maiden whom the angels name Lenore—
Nameless *here* for evermore.

And the silken, sad, uncertain rustling of each purple curtain
Thrilled me—filled me with fantastic terrors never felt before;
So that now, to still the beating of my heart, I stood repeating,
" 'Tis some visitor entreating entrance at my chamber door—
Some late visitor entreating entrance at my chamber door;—
This it is and nothing more."

Presently my soul grew stronger; hesitating then no longer,
"Sir," said I, "or Madam, truly your forgiveness I implore;
But the fact is I was napping, and so gently you came rapping,
And so faintly you came tapping, tapping at my chamber door,
That I scarce was sure I heard you"—here I opened wide the door;—
Darkness there and nothing more.

Deep into that darkness peering, long I stood there wondering, fearing,
Doubting, dreaming dreams no mortal ever dared to dream before;
But the silence was unbroken, and the stillness gave no token,
And the only word there spoken was the whispered word, "Lenore?"
This I whispered, and an echo murmured back the word, "Lenore?"
Merely this and nothing more.

Back into the chamber turning, all my soul within me burning,
Soon again I heard a tapping somewhat louder than before.
"Surely," said I, "surely that is something at my window lattice;
Let me see, then, what thereat is, and this mystery explore—
Let my heart be still a moment and this mystery explore;—
'Tis the wind and nothing more!"

Open here I flung the shutter, when, with many a flirt and flutter,

In there stepped a stately Raven of the saintly days of yore;
Not the least obeisance made he; not a minute stopped or
stayed he;
But, with mien of lord or lady, perched above my chamber
door—
Perched upon a bust of Pallas just above my chamber door—
Perched, and sat, and nothing more.

Then this ebony bird beguiling my sad fancy into smiling,
By the grave and stern decorum of the countenance it wore,
"Though thy crest be shorn and shaven, thou," I said, "art
sure no craven,
Ghastly grim and ancient Raven wandering from the Nightly
shore—
Tell me what thy lordly name is on the Night's Plutonian
shore!"
Quoth the Raven, "Nevermore."

Much I marvelled this ungainly fowl to hear discourse so
plainly,
Though its answer little meaning—little relevancy bore;
For we cannot help agreeing that no living human being
Ever yet was blessed with seeing bird above his chamber door—
Bird or beast upon the sculptured bust above his chamber
door,
With such name as "Nevermore."

But the Raven, sitting lonely on the placid bust, spoke only
That one word, as if his soul in that one word he did outpour.
Nothing farther then he uttered—not a feather then he fluttered—
Till I scarcely more than muttered, "Other friends have flown before—
On the morrow *he* will leave me, as my Hopes have flown before."
Then the bird said, "Nevermore."

Startled at the stillness broken by reply so aptly spoken,
"Doubtless," said I, "what it utters is its only stock and store
Caught from some unhappy master whom unmerciful Disaster
Followed fast and followed faster till his songs one burden
bore—
Till the dirges of his Hope that melancholy burden bore
Of 'Never—nevermore.' "

But the Raven still beguiling my sad fancy into smiling,
Straight I wheeled a cushioned seat in front of bird and bust
and door;
Then, upon the velvet sinking, I betook myself to linking
Fancy unto fancy, thinking what this ominous bird of yore—
What this grim, ungainly, ghastly, gaunt, and ominous bird
of yore
Meant in croaking "Nevermore."

This I sat engaged in guessing, but no syllable expressing
To the fowl whose fiery eyes now burned into my bosom's
core;
This and more I sat divining, with my head at ease reclining
On the cushion's velvet lining that the lamp-light gloated o'er,
But whose velvet-violet lining with the lamp-light gloating
o'er,
She shall press, ah, nevermore!

Then, methought, the air grew denser, perfumed from an
unseen censer
Swung by seraphim whose foot-falls tinkled on the tufted floor.
"Wretch," I cried, "thy God hath lent thee—by these angels
he hath sent thee
Respite—respite and nepenthe from thy memories of Lenore;
Quaff, oh, quaff this kind nepenthe and forget this lost
Lenore!"
Quoth the Raven, "Nevermore."

"Prophet!" said I, "thing of evil!—prophet still, if bird or
devil!—
Whether Tempter sent, or whether tempest tossed thee here
ashore,
Desolate yet all undaunted, on this desert land enchanted—
On this home by Horror haunted—tell me truly, I implore—
Is there—*is* there balm in Gilead?—tell me—tell me, I implore!"
Quoth the Raven, "Nevermore."

"Prophet!" said I, "thing of evil!—prophet still, if bird or devil!
By that Heaven that bends above us—by that God we both adore—
Tell this soul with sorrow laden if, within the distant Aidenn,
It shall clasp a sainted maiden whom the angels name Lenore—
Clasp a rare and radiant maiden whom the angels name Lenore."
Quoth the Raven, "Nevermore."

"Be that word our sign of parting, bird or fiend!" I shrieked, upstarting—
"Get thee back into the tempest and the Night's Plutonian shore!
Leave no black plume as a token of that lie thy soul hath spoken!
Leave my loneliness unbroken!—quit the bust above my door!
Take thy beak from out my heart, and take thy form from off my door!"
Quoth the Raven, "Nevermore."

And the Raven, never flitting, still is sitting, *still* is sitting
On the pallid bust of Pallas just above my chamber door;
And his eyes have all the seeming of a demon's that is dreaming,
And the lamp-light o'er him streaming throws his shadow on the floor;
And my soul from out that shadow that lies floating on the floor
Shall be lifted—nevermore!

Edgar Allen Poe

THE SADDEST WORDS

From Maud Muller

. . . . Of all sad words of tongue or pen,
The saddest are these: "It might have been!"

John Greenleaf Whittier

THE YEAR'S AT THE SPRING

The year's at the spring
And day's at the morn;
Morning's at seven;
The hillside's dew-pearled;
The lark's on the wing;
The snail's on the thorn;
God's in his heaven—
All's right with the world!

Robert Browning

UNDER THE GREENWOOD TREE

Under the greenwood tree
Who loves to lie with me,
And turn his merry note
Unto the sweet bird's throat,
Come hither, come hither, come hither:
Here shall he see
No enemy
But winter and rough weather.
Who doth ambition shun,
And loves to live i' the sun,
Seeking the food he eats,
And pleased with what he gets,
Come hither, come hither, come hither:
Here shall he see
No enemy
But winter and rough weather.

William Shakespeare

A THING OF BEAUTY

A thing of beauty is a joy forever;
Its loveliness increases; it will never
Pass into nothingness; but still will keep
A bower quiet for us, and a sleep
Full of sweet dreams, and health, and quiet breathing.

John Keats

HOW DO I LOVE THEE?

How do I love thee? Let me count the ways.
I love thee to the depth and breadth and height
My soul can reach, when feeling out of sight
For the ends of Being and ideal Grace.
I love thee to the level of everyday's
Most quiet need, by sun and candle-light.
I love thee freely, as men strive for Right;
I love thee purely, as they turn from Praise.
I love thee with the passion put to use
In my old griefs, and with my childhood's faith.
I love thee with a love I seemed to lose
With my lost saints—I love thee with the breath,
Smiles, tears, of all my life!—and, if God choose,
I shall but love thee better after death.

Elizabeth Barrett Browning

EPIGRAM

Sir, I admit your general rule,
That every poet is a fool,
But you yourself may serve to show it,
That every fool is not a poet.

Samuel Taylor Coleridge

ON THE GRASSHOPPER AND THE CRICKET

The poetry of earth is never dead:
When all the birds are faint with the hot sun,
And hide in cooling trees, a voice will run
From hedge to hedge about the new-mown mead;
That is the Grasshopper's—he takes the lead
In summer luxury,—he has never done
With his delights; for when tired out with fun
He rests at ease beneath some pleasant weed.
The poetry of earth is ceasing never:
On a lone winter evening, when the frost
Has wrought a silence, from the stove there shrills
The Cricket's song, in warmth increasing ever,
And seems to one in drowsiness half lost,
The Grasshopper's among some grassy hills.

John Keats

FABLE

The mountain and the squirrel
Had a quarrel;
And the former called the latter "Little Prig."
Bun replied,
"You are doubtless very big;
But all sorts of things and weather
Must be taken in together
To make up a year
And a sphere.

And I think it's no disgrace
To occupy my place.
If I'm not so large as you,
You are not so small as I,
And not half so spry.
I'll not deny you make
A very pretty squirrel track;
Talents differ: all is well and wisely put;
If I cannot carry forests on my back,
Neither can you crack a nut."

Ralph Waldo Emerson

INDEX OF TITLES

Animal crackers 220
Cat and the mouse in partnership, the 74
Christmas carol, a 78
Duck and the kangaroo, the 181
Epigram 248
Fable 250
Glorious whitewasher, the 56
How do i love thee? 247
In which pooh goes visiting and gets into a tight place 24
My early home 30
On the canal 14
On the grasshopper and the cricket 249
Pied piper of hamelin, the 140
Quangle wangle's hat 126
Raven, the 231
Reeds of innocence 219
Rip van winkle 152
River bank, the 185
Saddest words, the 243
Search for the wicked witch, the 38
Sorcerer's apprentice, the 130
Spider and the fly, the 228
Thing of beauty, a 246
Tom becomes a water baby 205
Tom takes becky's punishment 66
Twister a-twisting, a 226
Under the greenwood tree 245
Village blacksmith, the 222
Wise sayings from poor richard 120
Wreck, the 175
Year's at the spring, the 244

INDEX TO TITLES VOL. I TO IV

A

ALADDIN AND THE WONDERFUL LAMP, III 8
ALLIGATOR AND THE JACKAL, THE, III 210
ALPHABET FUN, I 151
ALPHABET RHYMES, I 232
ANDROCLES, II 152
ANIMAL CRACKERS, IV 220
ANT AND THE GRASSHOPPER, THE, II 150
APPLE PIE, I 66
AS I WAS GOING ALONG, I 87
AS I WAS GOING TO ST. IVES, I 40
AS TOMMY SNOOKS AND BESSY BROOKS WERE WALKING OUT ONE SUNDAY, I 201

B

BAA, BAA, BLACK SHEEP, I 62
BABY, I 242
BARBER, BARBER, SHAVE A PIG, I 94
BEAUTY AND THE BEAST, III 28
BED IN SUMMER, II 190
BELLING THE CAT, II 154
BIRDIES WITH BROKEN WINGS, II 246
BLOW, WIND, BLOW!, I 150
BOATS SAIL ON THE RIVERS, II 181
BOUNCE BUCKRAM, I 200
BOW, WOW, WOW, I 129
BOY'S SONG, A, II 182
BREMEN TOWN MUSICIANS, THE, III 143
BROW BENDER, I 226
BROWNIES TOBOGGANING, THE, II 89
BYE, BABY BUNTING, I 29

C

CALICO PIE, II 161
CAROL SINGERS, THE, II 128
CAT AND THE MOUSE IN PARTNERSHIP, THE, IV 74
CAT CAME FIDDLING OUT OF A BARN, A, I 177
CATERPILLAR, THE, II 239
CATS HAVE COME TO TEA, THE, II 221
CECILY PARSLEY, I 234
CHIMNEY, A, I 187
CHRISTMAS CAROL, A, IV 78
CINDERELLA, OR THE GLASS SLIPPER, III 16
CITY MOUSE AND THE GARDEN MOUSE, THE, II 177
CLOUDS, II 247
CLUCKING HEN, THE, II 250
COCK A DOODLE DOO, I 80
COCK, THE MOUSE, AND THE LITTLE RED HEN, THE, II 13
COLOR, II 189
THE COW (Jane Taylor), II 179
THE COW (Robert Louis Stevenson), II 200
CROSS PATCH, DRAW THE LATCH, I 98
CROW AND THE PITCHER, THE, II 149

D

DANCE, LITTLE BABY, DANCE UP HIGH, I 191
DING, DONG, BELL, I 64
DOG AND THE SHADOW, THE, II 148
DOG IN THE MANGER, THE, II 144
DRAKESTAIL, II 96
DREAM OF A GIRL WHO LIVED AT SEVEN-OAKS, THE, II 238
DUCK AND THE KANGAROO, THE, IV 181
DUEL, THE, II 222

E

ELIZABETH, I 231
ELVES AND THE CHANGELING, THE, III 99
EMPEROR'S NEW CLOTHES, THE, III 136
EPIGRAM, IV 248
ESCAPE AT BEDTIME, II 201

F

FABLE, IV 250
FAIRIES, THE, II 213
FARMER'S BOY, THE, I 116

FARMER WENT TROTTING, A, I 220
FIDDLE-DE-DEE, FIDDLE-DE-DEE, I 205
FIVE LITTLE FAIRIES, THE, II 244
FIVE LITTLE PIGS, I 142
FOR WANT OF A NAIL, THE SHOE WAS LOST, I 196
FOREIGN LANDS, II 197
FOX AND THE CROW, THE, II 143
FOX AND THE GOAT, THE, II 155
FOX AND THE GRAPES, THE, II 135
FOX AND THE STORK, THE, II 134
FROG HE WOULD A-WOOING GO, A, I 82
FROG PRINCE, THE, III 219

G

GEORGIE PORGIE, I 59
GLORIOUS WHITEWASHER, THE, IV 56
GOLDEN GOOSE, THE, II 82
GOOD-NIGHT, I 238
GOOSE WITH THE GOLDEN EGGS, THE, II 141
GOOSEY, GOOSEY, GANDER, I 60
GREAT A, LITTLE A, I 195

H

HANDY SPANDY, JACK-A-DANDY, I 88
HANSEL AND GRETEL, III 148
HAPPY THOUGHT, II 188
HARE AND THE TORTOISE, THE, II 158
HARK! HARK! THE DOGS BARK, I 208
HENNY-PENNY, II 22
HERE WE GO ROUND THE MULBERRY BUSH, I 56
HERE WE GO UP, UP, UP, I 144
HEY! DIDDLE, DIDDLE, I 36
HIAWATHA'S CHILDHOOD, II 194
HICKETY, PICKETY, MY BLACK HEN, I 41
HICKORY, DICKORY, DOCK, I 65
HISTORY OF TOM THUMB, THE, III 105
HORSES OF THE SEA, II 212
HOUSE THAT JACK BUILT, THE, II 55
HOW DO I LOVE THEE?, IV 247
HOW MANY MILES TO BABYLON?, I 32
HOW THE RAVEN HELPED MAN, III 216
HUMPTY-DUMPTY, I 78
HUSBAND WHO WAS TO MIND THE HOUSE, THE, III 130
HUSH-A-BYE, BABY, I 26

I

I AM A GOLD LOCK, I 178
I HAD A LITTLE DOGGY, I 194
I HAD A LITTLE HEN, THE PRETTIEST EVER SEEN, I 89
I HAD A LITTLE NUT TREE, I 79
I HAD A LITTLE PONY, I 134
I HARDLY EVER CRY, II 168
I LOVE LITTLE PUSSY, II 174
I LOVE SIXPENCE, PRETTY LITTLE SIXPENCE, I 198
I SAW A SHIP A-SAILING, I 76
IF ALL THE SEAS WERE ON SEA, I 174
IF A PIG WORE A WIG, I 227
IN WHICH POOH GOES VISITING AND GETS INTO A TIGHT PLACE, IV 24
INFANT JOY, I 246

J

JACK AND JILL, I 34
JACK AND THE BEANSTALK, III 87
JACK BE NIMBLE, I 77
JACK SPRAT, I 42
JACK THE GIANT KILLER, III 115
JENNY WREN FELL SICK, I 206
JOHNNY-CAKE, II 64
JOHNNY CROW'S GARDEN, I 99

L

LADY-BUG, I 149
LADY MOON, II 208
LAMB, THE, II 171
LAND OF THE COUNTERPANE, THE, II 205
LAND OF STORY-BOOKS, THE, II 202

LAUGHING SONG, II 170
LION AND THE MOUSE, THE, II 139
LION AND THE UNICORN, THE, I 124
LITTLE BETTY BLUE, I 140
LITTLE BO-PEEP, I 24
LITTLE BOY BLUE, I 58
LITTLE COCK-SPARROW, A, I 225
LITTLE ELF, THE, II 237
LITTLE GNOME, THE, III 254
LITTLE HOBBY-HORSE, THE, II 243
LITTLE JACK HORNER, I 53
LITTLE JOHN JIGGY JAG, I 95
LITTLE MAID, PRETTY MAID, WHITHER GOEST THOU?, I 115
LITTLE MISS MUFFET, I 27
LITTLE NANCY ETTICOAT, I 81
LITTLE POLLY FLINDERS, I 133
LITTLE RED RIDING-HOOD, II 33
LITTLE ROBIN-REDBREAST, I 147
LULLABY, I 247
LULLABY OF AN INFANT CHIEF, II 192
LULLABY, OH, LULLABY!, I 250

M

MAD TEA-PARTY, A, III 244
MAN IN THE MOON, THE, I 23
MAN IN THE WILDERNESS ASKED ME, THE, I 228
MARY'S LAMB, II 172
MILKMAID AND HER PAIL, THE, II 142
MISTRESS MARY, QUITE CONTRARY, I 33
MIX A PANCAKE, II 177
MONDAY'S CHILD IS FAIR OF FACE, I 215
MONTHS, THE, II 186
MOTHER, MAY I GO IN TO SWIM?, I 202
MRS. GOOSE'S STORE, II 72
MULTIPLICATION IS VEXATION, I 230
MY DEAREST BABY, GO TO SLEEP, I 240
MY EARLY HOME, IV 30
MY LITTLE OLD MAN AND I FELL OUT, I 90
MY SHADOW, II 198

N

NEEDLE AND THREAD, A, II 236
NEEDLES AND PINS, I 204
NIGHT, I 249
NORTH WIND DOTH BLOW, THE, I 132

O

OH! LOOK AT THE MOON, II 160
OLD KING COLE, I 50
OLD MAN AND HIS GRANDSON, THE, II 70
OLD MISTRESS MCSHUTTLE, I 91
OLD MOTHER HUBBARD, I 18
OLD WOMAN, THE, I 222
OLD WOMAN AND HER PIG, THE, II 26
ON THE CANAL, IV 14
ON THE GRASSHOPPER AND THE CRICKET, IV 249
ON YONDER HILL THERE STANDS A TREE, I 135
ONE, TWO, BUCKLE MY SHOE, I 71
OVER IN THE MEADOW, II 165
OWL AND THE PUSSYCAT, THE, II 226

P

PARADOXES, II 251
PEMMY, II 242
PETER, PETER, PUMPKIN-EATER, I 52
PIED PIPER OF HAMELIN, THE, IV 140
PINOCCHIO'S FIRST ADVENTURES, III 228
PIPER, THE, II 193
PIPES AND DRUMS, I 127
POPPY SEED CAKES, II 118
PUSS IN BOOTS, III 54
PUSSYCAT MOLE, I 138
PUSSY-CAT, PUSSY-CAT, WHERE HAVE YOU BEEN?, I 44

Q

QUANGLE WANGLE'S HAT, IV 126
QUEEN OF HEARTS, THE, I 46

R

RAIN, II 207
RAIN, RAIN, GO AWAY, I 176

RAPUNZEL, III 196
RAT AND THE ELEPHANT, THE, II 130
RAVEN, THE, IV 231
REAL PRINCESS, THE, III 76
REEDS OF INNOCENCE, IV 219
RIDE A COCK-HORSE, I 43
RIP VAN WINKLE, IV 152
RIVER BANK, THE, IV 185
ROBIN AND RICHARD, I 92
ROBIN THE BOBBIN, I 189
RUB A DUB DUB, I 183
RUMPELSTILTSKIN, III 50

S

SADDEST WORDS, THE, IV 243
SEARCH FOR THE WICKED WITCH, THE, IV 38
SEE A PIN AND PICK IT UP, I 188
SEE-SAW, MARGERY DAW, I 49
SEE-SAW SACRADOWN, I 96
SENSES, THE, I 139
SERVANT MAID AND THE ELVES, THE, III 100
SEVEN RAVENS, THE, II 113
SHEPHERD BOY AND THE WOLF, THE, II 136
SHOEMAKER AND THE ELVES, THE, III 96
SIMPLE SIMON, I 37
SING A SONG OF SIXPENCE, I 30
SING, SING, WHAT SHALL I SING?, I 148
SIX LITTLE MICE SAT DOWN TO SPIN, I 141
SLEEP, SLEEP, BEAUTY BRIGHT, I 248
SLEEPING BEAUTY, III 40
SLEEPY SONG, THE, I 244
SLEIGHBELLS, THE, I 126
SNOW WHITE, III 158
SOLOMON GRUNDY, I 145
SORCERER'S APPRENTICE, THE, IV 130
SPIDER AND THE FLY, THE, IV 228
STAR, A, I 186
STEADFAST TIN SOLDIER, THE, III 190
STITCHING, II 241
SUSAN BLUE, II 206
SWEET AND LOW, II 191

T

TABLE MANNERS, II 184
TAFFY WAS A WELSHMAN, I 184
TALE OF PETER RABBIT, II 50
TEENY-TINY, II 80
TEETH, I 93
THANKSGIVING DAY, II 228
THERE WAS A CROOKED MAN, I 190
THERE WAS A LITTLE GIRL, AND SHE HAD A LITTLE CURL, I 130
THERE WAS AN OLD MAN, AND HE HAD A CALF, I 180
THERE WAS AN OLD MAN OF TOBAGO, I 175
THERE WAS AN OLD WOMAN, AND WHAT DO YOU THINK?, I 197
THERE WAS AN OLD WOMAN LIVED UNDER A HILL, I 203
THERE WAS AN OLD WOMAN TOSSED UP IN A BASKET, I 131
THERE WAS AN OLD WOMAN WHO LIVED IN A SHOE, I 28
THERE WERE THREE JOVIAL HUNTSMEN, I 209
THERE WERE TWO BLACKBIRDS, I 143
THING OF BEAUTY, A, IV 246
THIRTY DAYS HATH SEPTEMBER, I 146
THIS LITTLE PIG WENT TO MARKET, I 72
THISTLE-SEED, I 223
THREE BEARS, THE, II 44
THREE BILLY GOATS GRUFF, THE, II 29
THREE LITTLE KITTENS, I 54
THREE LITTLE PIGS, THE, II 38
THREE WISE MEN OF GOTHAM, I 97
THREE WISHES, THE, II 110
TIME TO RISE, II 169
TINDER BOX, THE, III 78
TO MARKET, TO MARKET, I 224

TOM BECOMES A
WATER BABY, IV 205
TOM TAKES
BECKY'S PUNISHMENT, IV 66
TOM, TOM, THE PIPER'S SON, I 48
TOWN MOUSE AND THE
COUNTRY MOUSE, THE, II 146
TWEEDLEDUM AND
TWEEDLEDEE, I 182
TWENTY FROGGIES, II 248
TWINKLE, TWINKLE,
LITTLE STAR, II 176
TWISTER A-TWISTING, A, IV 226
TWO KEYS, I 192

U

UGLY DUCKLING, THE, III 176
UNDER THE
GREENWOOD TREE, IV 245
UPON A GREAT BLACK
HORSE-ILY, I 229
UPON MY WORD
AND HONOR, I 173

V

VELVETEEN RABBIT, THE, II 104
VILLAGE BLACKSMITH,
THE, IV 222
VISIT FROM
ST. NICHOLAS, A, II 230

W

WATER JEWELS, II 235
WEE WILLIE WINKIE, I 45
WHAT ARE LITTLE BOYS
MADE OF?, I 193
WHEN GOOD KING ARTHUR
RULED THIS LAND, I 216
WHEN I WAS A BACHELOR, I 181
WHEN LITTLE BIRDIE
BYE-BYE GOES, I 236
WHEN THE COWS
COME HOME, II 180
WHERE ARE YOU GOING,
MY PRETTY MAID?, I 218
WHERE THE BEE SUCKS, II 180
WHITTINGTON AND
HIS CAT, III 64
WHO HAS SEEN THE WIND, II 178
WHOLE DUTY OF
CHILDREN, II 204
WHY THE SEA IS SALT, III 202
WIND, THE, II 224
WIND AND THE SUN, THE, II 132
WISE SAYINGS FROM
POOR RICHARD, IV 120
WISHES, II 245
WISHING, II 216
WOLF AND THE CRANE,
THE, II 157
WOLF IN SHEEP'S
CLOTHING, THE, II 151
WOLVES AND THE
SHEEP, THE, II 156
WONDERFUL TAR BABY
STORY, THE, III 101
WOOLLY LAMBKINS, II 240
WORLD, THE, II 210
WRECK, THE, IV 175
WREN AND THE BEAR, THE, II 124
WYNKEN, BLYNKEN
AND NOD, II 218

Y

YEAR'S AT THE SPRING,
THE, IV 244